Vespasian Phantom is the talented author behind *"Unseen Cases of Detective Winston"*. While studying abroad, Phantom's passions for reading and writing flourish. Despite her youth, Phantom writes with remarkable depth and emotion. Her narratives take readers on thrilling journeys that provoke thought and evoke emotion. As Phantom continues to unveil her stories to the world, she aims to ignite a love for storytelling and kindle the flame of imagination in others.

To Mom and Dad, hope you're proud.

To Jackson Jones, for listening to my rambles for years.

And most of all, to my 16-year-old self, who spent hundreds of hours rewriting this.

Vespasian Phantom

UNSEEN CASES OF DETECTIVE WINSTON

AUSTIN MACAULEY PUBLISHERS™
LONDON • CAMBRIDGE • NEW YORK • SHARJAH

Copyright © Vespasian Phantom 2024

The right of Vespasian Phantom to be identified as author of this work has been asserted by the author in accordance with sections 77 and 78 of the Copyright, Designs and Patents Act 1988.

All rights reserved. No part of this publication may be reproduced, stored in a retrieval system, or transmitted in any form or by any means, electronic, mechanical, photocopying, recording, or otherwise, without the prior permission of the publishers.

Any person who commits any unauthorised act in relation to this publication may be liable to criminal prosecution and civil claims for damages.

This is a work of fiction. Names, characters, businesses, places, events, locales, and incidents are either the products of the author's imagination or used in a fictitious manner. Any resemblance to actual persons, living or dead, or actual events is purely coincidental.

A CIP catalogue record for this title is available from the British Library.

ISBN 9781035866236 (Paperback)
ISBN 9781035866243 (ePub e-book)

www.austinmacauley.com

First Published 2024
Austin Macauley Publishers Ltd®
1 Canada Square
Canary Wharf
London
E14 5AA

Table of Contents

Foreword	9
Chapter 1 Book Summary	10
Chapter 2 The Article	11
Chapter 3 Johannes	13
Two Months After the Disappearance	*14*
Chapter 4 10 Years	22
2003	*22*
2007	*24*
2016	*26*
Chapter 5 The Stranger in the Picture	28
20 March 2003	*28*
Chapter 6	41
Chapter 7 Unburied	42
Chapter 8 Writer in the Light	56
Chapter 9 3	71
Chapter 10 Doctor XZ	86

Chapter 11 Criminal Cleaner	101
Chapter 12 Guilty Widow	113
Chapter 13 Article	128
Chapter 14 144,000	130
Chapter 15 The Trial	145
Chapter 16 Sanning	159
Chapter 17 Dear Maxine	174
Chapter 18 Mötet	182
Chapter 19 Page 88	188
Chapter 20 The End	197
Chapter 21 Epilogue	205
Chapter 22 Final Article	206

Foreword

Dear reader, I am no detective—and this isn't New York, or the early 2000s or 2010s. This is Bexhill, a small charming village on the southern coast of England. I am 16—or was 16 perhaps. I have no idea when you are reading this book. I could be dead.

What matters is the story—or how I came up with this story. It was 2022 when I wrote my first word on a silly Microsoft Document. It had no title, no body and no end, but it was my first—I cherished it more than my firstborn child. What it lacked in literary skills, it made in the reaction I got from it. I was ecstatic.

And so, from 2022, I wrote.

And, on 3 August 2023, another document was opened on my Dell. And on that day, this story was born.

Chapter 1
Book Summary

130 cold-hearted killers caught. One still on the loose. Winston runs from his past until his time runs out. Through an archive of cold cases, he's closer to escaping than ever. As the investigation unfolds, we're caught in a web of lies and deception. This story follows a thin line between Winston's justice and his revenge.

The *Unseen Cases of Detective Winston* follows the story of Winston, who is introduced as a killer on trial for his crime. We follow him through 20 years of his career—following worldwide known cases like Criminal Cleaner or Unburied; we're torn between believing he's the good guy and seeing him as the cold-hearted killer he is. How long can Winston live on borrowed time?

Everything in Winston's life was running smoothly until he met Maxine Johannes. She was determined to find out the truth about Winston and his sinister past. Will she find out the truth before he's gone?

Chapter 2
The Article

11 April 2023
'Famous Detective Winston Faces Charges' Published by the *New York Times*

By: Charlotte Masar

We face corruption every day, but nothing could surprise New York more than the disappearance of Detective Winston, a world-renowned detective, who recently faced charges for a murder, which occurred almost three decades ago.

He was convicted as not guilty by the judge in September 2022. Many conspiracy theorists have said he disappeared because he was guilty after all, but the NYC police force is diligent not to let any details surrounding the murder trials get out. The entire NYC police force's reputation is at stake.

Detective Winston (54) was adored by many crime fans all over the world, with over 100 cases solved during his long career with the NYC police. We were unable to get any additional insights into the life of Detective Winston; his cell phone was left unanswered and his apartment is being sold as we speak. Maxine Mass has reportedly been suspended from her job as a detective on the NYC police force. The details as to why and when were not published.

Chapter 3
Johannes

Johannes
New York

"You know, I always wondered why you play that game with me." Maxine rolled around on the floor until she was facing Winston. He was in the middle of explaining the difference between two guns the force just confiscated last week. They were modified with a new barrel for better aim.

"What game?" Winston reached out with his two longest fingers to scoot the ashtray closer to him. He reached it and slowly moved it closer. The smell of cigarettes was embedded in the walls of his New York studio, but Maxine never complained. She always had a lighter in her pocket in case Winston forgot his own. She understood he thought better with a cigarette between his lips. She wondered if she would also be cleverer if she took up cigarettes.

"You always play that game. 'Guess which eye I'm looking into.' And I can never guess which one. I swear you're cheating and changing your answer." Maxine laughed as Winston lit up a cigarette and chuckled.

"I had a friend, a long time ago." Winston took a long drag of his cigarette—almost as if he enjoyed how the air

wasn't so crisp anymore and how his lungs burned after each drag.

"Shocking."

"He showed me how you can always tell when a person's lying." Winston licked his lips. "It doesn't matter how good they are at lying—every liar slips up sometimes."

"Not everyone. There are good liars there, you know? Like me, for example." Maxine ran a hand through her tangled hair.

"No, Maxine. Every liar will once get their karma."

"Imagine a world with no lies. Oh, how easy that would be. Everyone would just be happy and we could live our best lives." Maxine sighed.

"Everyone lies, Max. No matter how good you think they are, everyone lies. Some people just use small lies—complimenting people or making excuses. But one day, someone will tell you a big lie. Not just a small one—one that will change your life. And pray that day doesn't come because it will leave you desolate." Winston cast a small look towards Maxine, who was ready to crack a small joke. And then came reality.

Two Months After the Disappearance

The clock had been ticking off beat for the last 12 minutes. It kept ticking one millisecond sooner than the watch on my hand. I kept checking the time, wondering what could be taking so long.

I sat in complete silence—I was unsure if I should say something to Doctor Ashbery who sat opposite me. We were both waiting to be called in front of the commission hearing. He was supposed to be in there already, but Chief Kalman volunteered to go first and let us prepare our answers for longer.

I kept staring straight at the wall. I couldn't even look Ash in the eye. How pathetic.

"Stop staring at the wall," he grumbled and shuddered. The hallway was cold—colder than you'd expect. While the sun was shining outside and people wore shorts, we wore suits and shivered in this old building.

I thought about staying home, but then they would send two units to come pick me up. They learned after the last time. Ditching court wasn't as easy as ditching lessons at the academy.

It's been exactly three months after Winston vanished—or whatever his name was. I tried to get over it, but turns out that if people kept reminding you of someone, chances are you won't be able to forget them so easily. Each weekend, Carrie, Winston's ex-wife, knocked on my door and asked if he had reached out. She didn't know about the letter he sent me every 33 days.

It took approximately 33 days for a person to starve. He fed me one letter every 33 days so I wouldn't starve and die. Each day, I feared the next letter wouldn't come—that he had forgotten about me, or abandoned me. Perhaps I should stop reading them, but there is something so satisfying about knowing what he's up to. One month, he was drinking pure vodka from Russia, the next, he could be in the middle of the Arctic for all I know. He never told me where he was. Cop to a cop, he knew I would sit my ass on the next plane that was leaving JFK wherever he was.

Truthfully, it kept me up at night. I mean, who wouldn't be surprised that the perfect man I knew wasn't so perfect? The best cop I knew was a cold killer—we haven't even found the first body. How many are there? He was officially innocent—but which innocent person would run? And what's more frustrating, he knew exactly what I'd do and ask. It's like he saw me right through my window, banging my hands against the wall.

I was a control freak when I knew Winston. I used to know everyone and everything until the last detail. And then he left me the first letter and I had no idea what to do. He turned my life upside down within one week. I worked so hard to get where I am and he tore right through it. I had no ambitions; I couldn't get out of bed when last month I used to be up at six in the morning every day. I had no training partner, and what's worse, I lost my friend.

"I'm not staring. I'm admiring the wallpaper." I offered Ash a tight-lipped smile. What else could I say? Where else should I look? There was nothing in this building. The marble floors and walls were boring to look at. Sad beige colours engulfed me. I liked red, and Winston liked brown. Or was it just another lie?

Sometimes, I lay awake at night wondering if he was from the CIA or KGB and was sent to spy on me. Sometimes, I lay awake and hoped this was just a long nightmare and I would wake up and Winston would be standing next to my bed and would ask me which eyes he was looking into.

"I might be a mortician, and not a psychologist or therapist, but for the last two months, you've been off. And I know it's because he left, but you cannot waste time from your life thinking—overthinking—about Winston. No matter what scenario you'll come up with, it won't bring him back. He's gone, forever, period. Get a grip and live your life." He mumbled something at the end but I couldn't hear him. Perhaps I didn't want to hear what he had to say. Everyone magically knew what was wrong with me and how to fix it, but they hadn't even scratched the surface. Our relationship—obsession—went deeper than any relationship Winston had with his colleagues. I was his partner. They were just random people placed in the precinct.

"I'm not overthinking," I rolled my eyes, knowing he was right but still denying it.

"You know, this is exactly what he wants. He wants us to keep thinking about him. He wants to be remembered. He never could stomach being average, and this only fuels him and he knows it. Believe me. The best thing you can do is get over it and be better than him." He flipped a page of the *New York Times*, and there I saw it. The unruly article. I re-read it at least four times this morning.

"If I was better, or would be better, it would have to involve catching him. And as you said so many times, it's not likely that he will offer himself up just like that." I snapped my fingers in front of me.

Before Ashbery could come up with another metaphorical remark, Chief Kalman opened the door to the hearing room. He looked older than when he came in. His brows were creased and he wasn't cheery anymore. And if Kalman wasn't cheery, it only meant one thing—this hearing would be my last.

"Max, you're up," he mumbled quietly. I looked up at him and grabbed his shoulder before he could put his coat on and leave. "How bad?"

"Can't say, mine was worse than yours." He offered me an apologetic look as he fled through the front doors. I understood him and he understood me. Our pain was identical—almost.

I didn't look twice to know what was going on. They wanted to blame it on me, like three times before. But no matter what I would say today will change the fact that I'll go down in there—fighting for my life.

Commission hearings were my favourite before. You could flirt and roll your eyes as much as you'd want. There was no vocabulary you had to learn in order to sound professional. Most of the time, I kept quiet and complained under my breath, until I couldn't hold it inside of me anymore.

Entering the big hall, I nodded my head at the two judges I knew who sat in the high row. I sat down, bounced my leg, and offered my full attention to the men in front of me. If Winston was here, he'd whisper something funny in my ear to cheer me up—but he wasn't.

"Please state your full name for the record," the automated voice boomed loudly in the room full of silence.

"Maxine Regina Johanssen." I straightened my back to seem more composed.

"You're here for your partner, Detective Winston, so we will make this quick. Where is Detective Winston?"

"I have no idea. Same answer as the three times before." I shrugged—maybe I was giving them the impression that I helped the bastard escape.

"So, you had nothing—absolutely nothing—to do with the disappearance of Winston?" An older man whom I've never seen or heard about asked me with a snarl. Love your elders, kids, but elders won't ever respect you back.

"That is what I am declaring, yes. Tell me, how many times are you going to ask me the same questions? I have a nail appointment in less than an hour." I waved my hand in front of them and pursed my lips.

"Be respectful, Miss Johanssen."

"I will, when you stop wasting time on questioning me, and maybe shove all this lost time to trying find Winston." One of the men wanted to speak, but I waved my hand and stopped him. "And don't call him my partner, ever again. I have more than enough reasons to get up and leave without another word."

I had no reason to stay at my job for any longer, anyway. I was planning to pack my belongings and travel through the world to try and find him. The precinct only reminded me of him. The mahogany desk and the creaky chair. The dead plants that I refused to water—they were his responsibility, not mine.

"Calm down, Johannsen. We are trying to help." An older man coughed in the row and I could hear a small child crying outside. The cries weren't helping me to concentrate.

"Are you? So, this will help to bring him back and bring him to justice? Are we all in this room working to the same extent to find Winston? Because I've seen you, Senator," I pointed a finger in his direction, "I see how you enjoy your political life. I'm sure your wife would be disappointed if she found out about your flings. So, enjoy it while you can, because I will come for you and I'll make sure everyone knows that all of you men aren't doing anything to help search for a serial killer." The word tasted sour on my tongue, but it was fitting.

"This is why we called this hearing, Miss Johannsen. We were asked to monitor your mental condition. We were getting reports from your colleagues that your mental health is much damaged and perhaps you would need a longer leave of absence." I couldn't believe I was hearing these words. "We agreed that your work on the force shall be severed. Our choice won't change. You refused the therapy the precinct offered and you seem to have more anger issues than before."

The courtroom was silent. I could drop a pin and I'd hear it.

I could feel the whole world shaking—and it wasn't an earthquake. It was my hand holding onto the table with so much force, that I thought if I let go the table would be missing that wooden piece.

"No. I don't accept this decision." My voice broke midsentence. While I wanted to quit, I didn't want to quit now. The computers at the precinct would be helpful to find where Winston is hiding.

"Our decision is final. Your things will be delivered to your apartment by next week." The main speaker closed his file, and the lady typing on the computer hit the comma key. My career was over, just like that.

One thing Winston hadn't tarnished was now tarnished. My career was gone—I wonder if he was smiling or laughing wherever he was. I knew he knew. He was watching my moves. Maybe he didn't know I sensed that he was watching. He sent me a small postcard from Maldives last week, with the latest gossip from the precinct. He knew.

I stood up, chair flying behind me. I didn't spare one look at them or at the confused Ashbery. I needed to leave. I needed fresh air.

The whole room was spinning as I fled. If no one was going to bring Winston to justice, I gladly would.

I needed to find Winston and kill him myself.

This time, he wouldn't get away.

Chapter 4
10 Years

2003

"What's your name?" The redhead asked me. Her hair wasn't orange-red or copper; it was just red—red like blood, red like roses, or perhaps magnolias. I couldn't quite phantom why she was sitting in front of me, or why I was paying so much attention to her hair.

"Winston. I'm Detective Winston," I answered truthfully. Although I had a name, I didn't go by it. I was Winston—not Adam Winston, Jerry Winston, or Matt Winston—I was just Winston.

"My name is Maxine Regina Johannes." She held her head high, and I could hear a small Swedish accent escape from her perfect English.

"I'm sorry, who are you?" I cocked my head. I was told I would be meeting the star of the NY police academy, and I was sitting in front of a young girl.

When I first met you, Maxine, I had no idea you could be this greedy for knowledge. You strived to solve every, case, maybe even more than I did. I loved it. I felt younger every time you passed me in the halls. No matter how little our interaction was, I could feel you analysing my expression.

"Each of your wrinkles is like a scribble." She laughed. He made a funny face and she laughed even more.

I remember seeing you before you saw me.

I remember you looking over the computer in the library. You were so taken in by whatever was playing on the screen that you didn't notice me staring at you for almost an hour—but it felt like an eternity. I memorised every key you hit and knew exactly what you were writing. You were one of the brightest people I knew. But we all have our flaws.

Your flaw was that no matter how hard you tried to figure me out, you couldn't. Like a little mouse, you tried to follow me everywhere I went. You wanted in on my secrets.

I had so many secrets that I didn't know where to start.

"Remember, how I almost crashed your car all those years ago?" Maxine laughed so hard, a noodle escaped her mouth and fell on my carpet. She looked down on it, and looked up at me—I guess she expected me to be angry, but I just snorted and laughed.

"Don't laugh at me. I'm sorry for staining your carpet."

"Let's not act like it's brand-new." I pointed to a stain from my cat Luther, who loved to piss me off by leaving his dirt on my carpet.

"The real question is, do you remember when we had that new detective come in and you spilt coffee all over his brand-new sweater?" I teased Maxine.

The new detective was me, and she almost gave me a heart attack with that burn. It's almost healed now. I can still see my skin is a little red from the edge of that burn—a constant reminder of Maxine.

2007

"Is it okay if I ask you a question?" Maxine pondered, sitting in the passenger's seat of my Ford.

"You just did," I smirked a little—she was always so shy when she asked me things. I felt our generation gap in music, the way she talked, and all the movies she watched that I'd never heard of. Star Wars was too new for me. I liked the older classics.

"Why don't you have a name?" From my peripheral vision, I could see her playing with her nails. She was constantly aware of how her hands looked. One day she told me how she hated to shake hands because of how small her hands were—how it reminded her that she would never fill the role of a detective. I assured her that I would be the one who shook hands. I never broke my promise. Each time someone raised their hand, I made sure to shake it before they even offered it to Maxine.

"I do have a name, you know. I just don't use it." I sped alongside cars.

"Why not? Is it ugly?"

"Are you interested in possible future baby names?" I teased. I brought in Maxine's boyfriend at least once a week to the station. He dealt drugs. But no one can stop 'love'—at least that's what Maxine told me.

"Fuck off." She punched my shoulder and slouched in her seat. I could see something was bothering her, but I felt that I shouldn't ask. I wasn't someone you could tell all your worries to.

"Why did your mother name you Maxine?" I looked at her.

"It means 'The Greatest'. She was a poet and thought I could follow in her footsteps and become the new generation, Plath. She was a little delusional sometimes." Maxine chuckled. I knew Maxine had a hard relationship with her mother, but I pretended not to notice, for her sake.

After a moment of silence, I could feel her slowly drifting away.

Maxine looked out of the window, contemplating what to say. "My name is Rain."

"That's a beautiful name—Rain Winston." Maxine tasted it on her tongue and smiled silently. "Why Rain?"

"When I was born, it was the rainiest day in the whole year. As I was born, the rain intensified so much that my mother said only my cries tore her sight away." I smiled at the memory of her.

"That's good. I hate when people give children names without meaning. It's almost like they didn't have nine months to come up with something meaningful." Maxine rolled her eyes. I shook my head, surprised. I never noticed Maxine paid so much attention to the details.

"Do you think we will be partners?" She suddenly asked.

"I don't know. I hate to think that far." I chuckled and noticed her watching me intensively. She wanted a reaction out of me.

"I hope we're not. You're annoying," she joked.

"Yeah. So old, right?" I pretended to twirl my hair.

"So old." Maxine laughed and I could see a small spark of excitement in her eyes—maybe the future wouldn't be so bleak.

2016

"You think they're going to fire you?" Maxine's lip wobbled.

With worry, her takeout box was untouched on my dining table.

"Hope not." I took in a deep breath to try and clear my mind. We just lost a new serial killer, who had killed two families inside of their homes. Chief Kalman was on my ass ever since I started this case, and my selfishness helped him escape—I didn't let Maxine lead and now he was running wild all over Nebraska.

"Don't joke about this."

I tried to help the situation with my positive tone, but Maxine didn't seem to appreciate it.

"I'm sorry, kid. I didn't mean it like that."

"I know. I just wished you weren't so careless about this. We're a family, Winston. I don't want you to get fired—where would I get another partner?"

"Don't worry. There are plenty of men on this force."

"None of them are you," she continued. "None of them are so careless and selfish and so funny and smart. I'm lucky I got you," Maxine confessed. We were never the kind of people who took feelings seriously, but she was making my heart squeeze.

I hated this. I hated the fact that I couldn't tell her who I really was. I hated that every time I looked at her, all I could imagine was how her face would look like when she realised she would have to catch me and put me behind bars one day. I hated that she looked at me for clarity, while all I could give her was a cheap lie.

"They won't separate us. But you have to be wise, Maxine. It's not all about us." I tried to make her understand, but she was looking at me as if I just broke her heart.

"It is all about us."

"That's selfish."

"I hope it is. I'm standing next to the most selfish man who ever existed." She smirked.

And God, was she right?

Chapter 5
The Stranger in the Picture

20 March 2003

It was early March 2003. I was working on one of my first real detective cases alone, without an additional supervisor to monitor me. I was called into Exeter, close to Appalachia. I had no friends or co-workers there—I was completely alone, driving on the highway in my car, blasting Susan Vega, and silently signing.

Even though Appalachia seemed beautiful, I heard all the stories surrounding the area. The scratches and the children's cries at night, the howls and the people appearing in your kitchen window. It scared me shitless. But what I wasn't prepared for was this case.

As a young man and a pretty new detective on the force, I wasn't nearly ready to read the initial coroner's report. Doctor Ashbery let me take a brief look at the pictures of the body, but I didn't even last a few seconds looking.

A seven-year-old boy was found beaten to death in the middle of the mountains. His mother, who single-highhandedly raised him, had no idea who could've done it. This case had been sitting in the archives for years now. I felt, that each time I came to the archives, hundreds of more unsolved cases made it there. I felt the immense need to solve all of them.

I arrived next to a small cottage, entirely made from wood. It had two small windows, and I could see a woman chopping wood in the back. Her back was hunched, her skirts dirtied with mud. She looked old, but at the same time younger than me.

"Ma'am," I greeted her, tipping my hat to the front. She turned around, and as I expected, she didn't sound a day over 30.

"Are you the new sheriff?" Her voice was meek, like a mouse's. "No, ma'am, I'm from New York. I saw your case and decided to re-open it," I announced. She let out a small chuckle, and it made me feel eerie.

"Come inside. I will answer your questions." She threw the axe away from herself and let it fall freely to the ground. She had long dark hair, raven-coloured, but her whole face was drained of colour.

I looked around as I entered the house. No pictures, no television, and no phone line. She didn't even have an oven she lived as off-grid as the state allowed her to. We sat down behind a small wooden table. The whole house was made of wood and it looked as if she built it.

"How long have you been living here?" I questioned.

"14 years." She gulped as she answered. I did the math in my head. She was too young to have the child, or was I wrong about her age?

"How old are you, ma'am?" I interjected. She looked both old and young, at the same time. Without noticing, she put a small copper cup in front of me with herbal tea.

"34. I thought you knew stuff like this from all the files," she remarked. I bit back a small huff. What a woman!

"No, ma'am. These files are too old. They need some updating," I retorted, but I pulled out my stack of files anyway. They had a big coffee stain on the front, as well as the pages waving. "The filing standards have changed." I cleared my throat, taking a sip from the steaming cup.

"So, please take me through what happened that night." I made myself as comfortable as possible on the wooden chair, which dug into my back. My knees bumped into the table, but when she started speaking, I opened my diary and scribbled some notes.

"My son and I used to do everything together. From waking up to cooking—you can imagine. He grew up without a father, and I refused to let him grow up to be like his father." She paused for a second but resumed talking. "It was November when it happened. The nights were cold, and my son knew how I hated it when he left to go out without me. You probably heard the stories…" I nodded my head and underlined a sentence in my notes. "I put him to sleep in his room. I tried teaching him some individuality, but I missed him soon after laying down in my bed. So, I went into his room and I found out that the comforter was cold and he wasn't anywhere in the house. I panicked and ran outside. I searched for a few minutes, but it was so cold. I came back inside and prayed to God that he was still alive." She took a tissue and blew out her nose.

"Where is his father now?" I could see she was uncomfortable with my question.

"He left two years after my son was born. He was not meant to be a father in the first place."

"Do you have any neighbours?" I looked up from my notebook to find her still sniffling.

"None. The nearest person who lived here died a couple of years ago. I'm all alone here. The cops said they cannot solve a murder without any suspects." She stuffed the dirty tissue into one of the pockets of her skirt.

"Did you kill him? Your son?" I inquired, but all I heard was a stammer.

"Detective Winston, I am a mother. Mothers feel nothing but love towards their children, and I am also a woman of God. I would never harm another human like that," she exclaimed.

My diary held three sentences.

Does the mother kill her son?
Does an animal kill a child?
Someone is hunting here?

When I first saw the pictures, I almost got into a fight with the chief, pushing forward the idea that this was a normal animal killing. Three medical examiners said this was not, in fact, an animal killing. They all found gunshots, instead of teeth marks or scratches.

Now, asking a mother if she killed her son turned up empty.

My sub consciousness agreed with my theory; she was innocent. "Do you by any chance own a gun or a hunting rifle?"

"No, sir. I hate guns." She coughed. I could see she was sick. Was it genetic?

And the only thing that was left was a third person. A hunter, perhaps or a ranger who accidentally shot a child instead of an animal. But four bullets were no accident.

I did not leave the hut alone afterwards. I was camping outside in my car. I felt a chill run down my spine when one of the tree branches hit my window. I was parked a few hundred metres away; I said goodbye to the mother and promised I'd be back tomorrow. Her case kept getting more and more interesting.

I took my shoes off and put my seat down to at least rest my eyes for an hour or two. Sleeping in my car in a forest somewhere in Appalachia was dangerous, but I wanted to monitor her. This whole case didn't make any sense. How could a murder happen when there was no one present?

I was on the verge of falling asleep when a bullet hit my car door.

I was more awake than ever, grabbing my gun and straightening my back to shoot at whoever just shot at me. "Fucking hell," I mumbled, but as I prepared to shoot, I looked out of the window, and all I could see were dense trees. I gulped, waiting to hear and feel another shot, but nothing came. The sky was starting to darken, and my senses were filled with fear and anxiety. I started my car and slammed the brakes, reversing out of the small dirt path I found. Looking back at the house, I wondered if the mother heard the shot.

Nevertheless, the fact that I was being shot at, made no progress in this case. I had no murder weapon; I had no suspect and the mother was no help. I could see that she wanted to solve this case as much as I did, lay her son at rest with God, and live the rest of her life in peace. But something was off.

The house looked too clean, too unused. If you compared it to my apartment, this place would seem like a model house. There was no dust, no scratches, and no evident dirt. In a place like this, how could you be so clean? It wasn't just the house. It was also the woman. She wore clothing that must've been older than her; she was only in her 30s but looked to be 45. Her hands were clean, even from chopping wood, she had no rough callouses or any scratches. She lived completely off the grid—in this century that seemed unbelievable. No cable and no television? Does she also knit in her free time? Why did she choose to live like this? I could see and hear from her cough that her health was declining. Maybe that's why she was so helpful in the first place—a dead woman cannot help her dead son more than a living woman.

Arriving back at the station, I made a bed out of the small couch. I was too tired to go sleep in a motel, and too afraid at the same time.

I went over the case once again, writing down anything strange that made me question this case. I closed my eyes and played the images together.

A small boy running away.

A man following him.

A small interaction, perhaps he asked who the boy was, but the boy was too young to reply.

The man was now mad because he got no answer.

He shot the boy.

A small siren went off in my head.

The boy wasn't shot at close range. He was shot from a few yards. 23 yards to be exact. I realised I needed to see the crime scene again. And I needed to take the mother with me.

The next morning, I found her chopping wood again. She wore the same clothing, had the same hairstyle, and greeted me the same way as yesterday. She seemed unreal—almost like a hologram.

"Morning," she chirped. A rancid smell of gas made my face scrunch.

When she saw my expression, she ushered me to come inside the hut. "I'm sorry; I'm just burning some old furniture. Come inside." She led the way to her front door, but I interrupted her before she could come inside.

"I want you to come with me. I'm going to the scene of the crime." I was determined to get her to go with me.

"Why?" She quietly replied. "Do you want me to see it to feel pain?" A pang of pain hit my chest. She seemed hurt by my request, but I needed her to come with me.

"Your son saw something in that place, that's why he left in the middle of the night. I need to know what he saw, and who is better to help me than you, his mother?" I offered her the stack of files. "This is me being honest. I need your help. I know everyone treated you like you're a wounded animal but I know you knew him best. So, help me to find his killer so we can both get some nice sleep tonight." I held out the files for her to take. I could see she was deep in thought. She took the files and held them to her chest.

I turned around, not expecting an answer. I hoped she would follow me into my car, and she did. She even muttered a 'thank god' before getting into the car. I motioned for her to put on a seat belt and she obliged.

We drove for almost 10 minutes in pure silence. She kept playing with one of the layers of her skirt, and I kept my eyes on the road. I put the car into park and opened my door; she mimicked my actions and got out. Looking around herself, she mumbled a few words before we both started walking, I in the direction of the map, and she the opposite way. I looked back over my shoulder and saw her looking into the forest as if someone was standing there.

"You coming?" She jumped but nodded her head and started to run after me. It was like she saw a ghost. Maybe she saw her little child running towards her. Visions of dead people weren't uncommon for the families of the victims.

"What did you see?" I asked her when she stopped running and stood next to me.

"Nothing." She brushed off my gaze and kept walking faster and faster until she was in front of me. Then, like clockwork, she stopped. In the middle of the tall grass, she stopped and breathed in.

"This is it," I spoke up after a few seconds of looking at her.

"I know." She crouched down to feel the ground, and I stood over her. I might think I know it all, but I could never fake the connection between a mother and a child—and the infinite bond between them.

"How long did he lay here before you found him?" She asked and I kept quiet.

"How long, detective? You owe me that." I opened my mouth to speak but closed it. "Nine hours."

"Nine hours," she repeated and wiped her cheek with her white sleeve.

"You know, someone must've killed him. It wasn't an animal attack, that we know for sure. Someone was here, hunting or shooting for fun. They hit him, and it wasn't an accident. They fired four bullets. Not one, not two, but four,"

I reminded her. "So, if you have any, any idea, a person's name, an old friend, or maybe someone who wished you ill, please tell me, and I will question them." I examined her reaction, but all I could see was sadness and remorse.

"There's no one. I had no family, no friends, and no neighbours. The whole village is too far and I knew no one." She straightened her back, and before I could protest, she brushed beside me and walked back, straight into my car.

"Take me home, Detective. And please, drop this case. I had enough," she mumbled before looking outside of the window, and not speaking for the rest of the ride.

"I will." That was my last word before I started the car and drove away.

One thing you should know about me is that I did not intend to keep my promise. I kept my distance for exactly two days before my willpower ran out and I yet again drove miles to the cabin.

After looking back on my decisions in this case, I realise that there was something more than the desire to solve it. I suddenly grew emotional towards the dead child. The academy teaches you what emotions you should be feeling, but when I saw the picture of a small child, his stomach shot up, leaving just enough tissue to connect him to his other limbs, I almost cried. And more, I felt anger towards his mother. Who lets their child outside at night? I wanted to hate her, but something in my gut told me that she was innocent in this after all. She had no alibi, but no motive to kill her child after all.

But who the hell did then?

I turned off the car's motor and slowly but steadily crept toward the cabin. No lights were turned on inside, but it was only 5, so I imagined her knitting in front of the fireplace.

My boots crunched the leaves underneath them. It had rained last night, so the ground was wet and mushy. A sudden image of the dead boy flashed inside my mind and I had to rub my eyes to get rid of it.

I finally came close enough to the door to see the door was opened. The small opening was abruptly closed due to the wind. I stifled but decided to open the door anyway. Coming inside, I closed the door behind me and breathed in the smell of rain, mixed with the smell of burning wood. I saw the fireplace had only one plank of wood left, the flame dancing, but getting smaller and smaller by the second until it disappeared. I don't know how long I've been standing here, but the feeling of déjà vu took over me.

I walked around, aiming to go investigate the kitchen to see if this woman had any guns when a floorboard creaked. I brushed it off, but an eerie breeze of air creeping through the window stopped me. I turned around, crouched, and tried to locate which plank of wood creaked. My hands kept brushing over the wood until I shifted my weight towards one plank and it creaked.

"Finally." I let out a breath I didn't know I was holding. I dug my nails into the side of the wood plank, shifting it slightly. But I struggled. The wood piece was heavy and my nails weren't long enough to help me lift it.

I was almost on the verge of giving up when the piece of wood finally lifted. I blew on my fingers to distract myself from the pain caused. I was sure I had wooden splinters underneath my nails, but it didn't matter, because when I laid the plank of wood beside me, something a few metres underneath me glimmered. I lay down, cheeks pressed against the wood and I tried to reach it. I prayed my hands were long enough—and they were. I hooked my finger in a hole and grabbed it. The silver glow of the revolver 657. I knew this one by the weight and the handle, a collector's piece almost.

But then my eyes caught another thing. A piece of photo paper shines underneath the dimmed lights. I reached again, but I couldn't reach it now. I rose to my knees and dialled the number to the station. A secretary answered, and I almost shouted at her to send me some backup. I completely filtered out the mother, not caring if she was going to see me. She was already in deep shit for lying to me. I almost got played by her, but my gut screamed at me until I finally rose from my office chair and grabbed my keys.

In less than twenty minutes, I heard the voice of my temporary colleague scream. "Detective!" I was waiting on the steps leading to the cabin, holding a wet picture in my hands.

The picture held a mother and her child, but on the right side stood a man, presumably the father. The photo had a date, a year before the son's murder. I led my team inside to bag the gun and the photo. Standing over the crouching technician I couldn't help, but wonder.

Could a parent kill their child?

The true answer never came. We organised a search for the mother and father but found no one. That was until a few weeks after the case, we found a woman hanging in the middle of the forest, only wearing a shirt and no skirt.

This is what I imagine happened; the mother tried to play me and thought she succeeded, but then two days later, I showed up, parking my car close enough to the house that she could see me. She had no time to take any of her things, so she ran, almost naked to the forest. I presume she wanted to meet with her husband somewhere out of town because at the cabin, we found three bags packed full of clothes, a couple of diaries fully written, and her sewing kit. It came as no surprise to me when I saw that the only thing she had on herself was a rosary, with her child's name written on the side of it. We had no idea who the husband was, tried running him through all the systems but he never appeared. We stood on all the sides of town, checking vehicles and vans leaving and arriving, but I was sure enough that if he was ever here, he was long gone.

A week after, the crime made the headline again after all these years; a tech came into my office and gave me her two diaries.

They told me the rest of the truth I was searching for.

A few years before the murder, both parents got married, unofficially in their barn. The marriage was organised by their parents, who were in debt and needed to tie themselves to another family to be able to pay off debts and mortgages. They soon had a child, but he seemed to be on the spectrum. This always angered the father, because he wanted a strong son to help with the cabin. They of course tried for other kids but never succeeded. The mother wrote that her husband turned out to be abusive, and always hit her son when he couldn't answer his questions or help to set up the table. At such a young age, he took him to 'hunt' in the forest. Turns out, they weren't hunting for animals. The father quickly grew angry at the son and told him to watch out for deer, while he took the high ground and shot his son four times. He came back into the cabin and told the mother her son wasn't coming back. She thought it was an animal attack, but then the police came knocking on the door, and the husband bolted. She was left alone to grieve her dead son and her missing husband. He was never registered, which is why we couldn't find him. He lived off the grid and for years, never returned.

Sometimes I wonder if I will ever have kids, and then remember that evil people exist and change my mind.

The mother couldn't handle living with the guilt and lies, so she took her own life. Even her religion couldn't stop her.

Now at least, they could meet and she could tell him all the stories she didn't have time to share in their time here. She could hug him again, without crying salty tears. I hope her husband is far away from my reach because if not, I swear I might send him right down to hell.

Now I know that a parent can kill their child.

Chapter 6

Detective Winston: A Legacy of Great Achievements in Law Enforcement
Published by *The New York Times*

By: Charlotte Masar

In the realm of law enforcement, certain individuals rise to prominence due to their exceptional skills, dedication, and unwavering commitment to justice. Detective Winston stands as a shining example of such an individual, having carved out a legacy of great achievements throughout his illustrious career. From solving complex cases to fostering community relations, Detective Winston's contributions have left an indelible mark on the field of criminal investigation.

One of Detective Winston's most notable achievements lies in his remarkable record of solving high-profile and seemingly unsolvable cases. His keen analytical mind, attention to detail, and tenacity in pursuing leads have consistently led to the successful resolution of criminal investigations. Colleagues and superiors commend Detective Winston for his ability to connect the dots, unravel intricate plots, and bring perpetrators to justice.

Chapter 7
Unburied

Unburied
28 June 2005

My summers weren't filled with vacations—quite the opposite. I worked every single day of the summer. Even on weekends, I would take long strides to the office; I would make the same coffee, and drink it on the same chair. I liked the routine it brought to each day. No days were simple, but none were extraordinary—that was, until the end of June 2005.

I could see children walking to school; some were already being driven home by their parents. I parked my Ford into my usual parking space when I saw my undergrad student already waiting for me, holding the door open. I speed walked to meet here and there. "We have a problem," she simply stated.

Maxine was assigned to me almost three months ago. We made a good team, mainly because she was still a bit afraid of me.

"What's the problem, kid?" I asked, already craving my coffee. She handed me a steaming mug of cinnamon goodness and walked in front of me.

"We got a murder."

"Is that supposed to be unusual?" I joked, straightening my back as I walked into the crowded and loud building. She didn't laugh.

"Listen to this; this morning, we found a body and instead of one perp, we got three."

I gave her a confused look. "Three people?"

"Three people confessed, saying the same story, word for word. Is that still funny?" She gave me an uncomfortable nod, signalling for me to cut my jokes and focus on the case.

"Three? Three people confessing to one murder?" I was shocked.

In my 20 years of practice, I almost always had a problem finding even one suspect—but now I had three. Walking into my office, I saw the three pictures of the people.

They almost stared at me.

"Victim is, well, was buried already. It's an older man, who died in the year 2000 and was buried for almost five years untouched." Maxine moved around my office, grabbed a pile of papers, and sat them on my lap.

She is fast, I'll give her that.

A few seconds later, I set my empty cup down. "Motive?" I opened the first file, and it looked like a normal woman. No previous hassle with the law, she had had two grown children, and worked a steady job at an office. The next suspect was an older man, with grandchildren, retired. The third suspect was a teenage girl, she didn't even have a driving licence, yet she already dug up a body.

"None. No one knew the man or knew someone who knew the man." Maxine sat down next to the window, the light illuminating her figure.

"Why is this case on my table if there is no murder?" I quizzed Maxine, my voice laced with annoyance.

"That's the thing. They were all in the middle of a cornfield with bloody clothes, with dirty nails and everyone kept saying they killed someone. We took them in for questioning, and each one said the exact same story, word for word." This case officially became interesting enough for me to pay attention.

"And?" I pushed Maxine to speak further.

"Three random suspects, who don't know each other, and never even heard each other's names, ended up killing the same person? Isn't that a bit strange?" She sat down in front of me, and I closed my eyes, imagining the three suspects killing a fourth, random person.

"Tell me more, kid, details." Maxine knew how my brain functioned. I needed as much information as possible to understand the case—I wanted to get into the head of the murderer and understand them.

"Teenage girl said she was the one who stabbed our victim. She felt the need to stop his heart."

"Was she on drugs?" I was grasping, guessing what could've happened.

"No drugs, no alcohol, not even weed. The tox screen said they were clean." Maxine blinked before I started playing with my hands, and continued to speak.

"The victim has not been found yet. That can mean that maybe this is some prank." I put my hands behind my head and lifted my boots to lie on the conference table.

"Put your feet down, you might be old, but you're not that old." Maxine rolled her eyes and kicked my feet off the table.

"Are you 23, or 40? Remind me, I keep forgetting." I smirked as she rolled her eyes again.

"Grandpa was the one with blood underneath his nails. But the blood doesn't match anyone in our database, and it's not animal blood. Lab tested it and said they cannot find whose blood this is." I wanted to ask if it was animal blood, but Maxine seemed to be reading my mind today.

"I need proof. I need something solid, Max. You know it." I sighed. I wanted to solve this case but without solid evidence—fingerprints, or hairs, or something that can point to one person—I couldn't.

"Are three suspects not enough?" She knitted her eyebrows together and a small crease formed in her forehead. She was getting impatient now.

"The other woman, Jessica, says she remembers absolutely nothing." Seems like her drugs are already gone.

I tried to remember the list of drugs that can make you hallucinate and that you can cook at home, but my mind seemed to be occupied with another thought. Three suspects and no dead body.

"Bring Jessica into the interrogation room. I want to talk to her myself." I stood up, opening my second drawer for my special notebook.

"Can I come too?" Maxine asked, and I nodded my head yes.

"We will be waiting for you." Maxine's last words rang in my head. *'We will be waiting'* seems to haunt me these days. A small flashback tries to pry me off work, but I push it back into the abyss of my mind.

Jessica was in her mid-30s. She wore a grey suit as if she was ready to go to work. Her wallet and ID were on the steel table in front of her. I could see the dried blood on her hairline, mixing in with the copper tone of her hair.

"Good morning, Miss Valene. I'm Detective Winston. I need to know what happened yesterday." My chair made a scraping sound as I dragged it away from the table. We had no time for mind games, so I just got straight to the point.

"I swear I didn't do any drugs, I-I'm a mother, please." Jessica's eyes watered and she blew her nose out into a used tissue. I could already read her. She pretended to be a good mother, but I could see her drinking cheap wine out of the largest wine glass she could find in Target. She might hate her husband and her life, but she didn't hate anyone enough to kill them.

"Jessica, please calm down," Maxine said, standing behind me with a clipboard in her hands.

"I know you didn't do any drugs." I truly didn't, but I needed to calm her down. "Tell me what is the last thing you remember? We can go from there." I handed her another tissue.

"The last thing I remember was around 7, last night. I was just putting my laundry into the washing machine, and then I was standing in the middle of the field with two strangers staring at me. I have no idea what could've happened. I didn't drive my car anywhere, but I live miles away from that cornfield," she confessed while heaving.

I looked over at Maxine, and she shook her head, signalling what Jessica said was true. Now there were three confused people, with sudden memory loss and one dead body—still at large.

"Did you eat or drink anything special before 7?" I asked. Jessica looked at me with a puzzled expression. "I need to make sure you weren't poisoned with a toxin or a drug. Maybe you didn't even notice, but you could've digested it. Nothing showed up in the toxicology report, but it might have been a modified drug that's unknown to us. You could've even breathed it in," I explained.

"I drank my regular coffee when I was returning from work; I stopped for it in a small cafe. I can give you the address if you want. But I need to know—did we hurt someone?" Her eyes pleaded for an answer. She almost looked sorry.

"There is no body," I answered, slowly rising from my seat.

"Yet," I added, leaving the room, and letting Maxine deal with Jessica, whose tears were escaping and her shoulders were trebling.

Walking back towards my office, I could see a white van with the news logo standing outside the precinct. *Great*, I thought. That's just peachy.

Jessica's lawyer arrived, and so did the teen's. No one came for the older man. I wondered if it was him, perhaps, who organised this rave. He sat in a chair, in the corner, and didn't utter one word ever since I started monitoring him through the interrogation window. He never made eye contact with the two women, and it looked like he was chanting a prayer.

"Winston." Maxine stood behind me, arms crossed and a hard look on her face. Maxine sometimes looked tougher than I did. She was a bad ass woman, and one day I hoped I could call her my partner.

"Maxine." I nodded for her to come closer. "What do you think?" I nodded toward the older man.

"I think he's scared for his life. He seems to be religious. Maybe we should grill him first," she answered honestly. I liked Maxine, mostly because of her sharp tongue and honesty. She never lied or pretended to be someone else. She was confident in her choices and never seemed to be quiet. "Get him in a room," I silently commanded, wondering if it was a good choice.

In less than ten minutes, me and Maxine were sitting in front of Bradley. Bradley was 72 years old, a small-town farmer, and lived the closest to the cornfield he was found in.

"Bradley, what did you do yesterday? Anything special?" I challenged his silence, but was only met with a mutter of 'nothing'.

"Mr Bradley, please understand we are trying to help you. There is still a possibility you were involved in a crime," I didn't finish my sentence because Bradley interrupted me.

"I was violated," he whisper-shouted. "I am the victim here; do you not see that? I was taken from my home and dumped in the middle of a cornfield with those two women." His tone changed suddenly. "I was almost killed? Wasn't I?" He asked me. Maxine scoffed from her seat.

"Mr Bradley, you may have a dead person's blood on your hands. You are a suspect in a crime, not the victim. Stop pretending you are so hurt and start answering some questions, otherwise, we will charge you tonight, and you can say goodbye to your farm." Maxine hummed reassuringly in a tone that sometimes scared even me. After an unsatisfying grilling, I and Maxine left the room.

"Maybe he's right," I replied, looking at Maxine. She raised her eyebrows in a challenging manner. "These three, they're not criminals. They're normal people. What if someone targeted them? It's not so unlikely," I added. I could see the fire in Maxine's eyes burning. This girl needs some anger management class.

"Do you by any chance go to a coffee shop in the city?" I offered Bradley a tight-lipped smile.

"Hell, no," he replied and scoffed as if I offended him.

And right there, the only possible lead we had was gone. Just like that.

The next morning was the same as the last. Maxine was waiting for me at the door; she rushed me through her case notes, but one sentence stopped me dead in my tracks.

"What did you say? Repeat that," I said, cursing as she bumped into me while turning to face me.

"All of them swear they acted alone," she replied sarcastically.

Three murderers. One body.

Three murderers. Three bodies.

"Get me all three of them in an interrogation room," I said as I ran to my office and grabbed the same notebook as yesterday. Descending the stairs, I saw our three suspects sitting close to each other in the room. They all looked extremely tired—their hair was greasy, their clothes unwashed and their appetite for answering questions was lower than before. Opening the door to the interrogation room, Maxine's hand shot up to stop me. "Do you think it was them?" This was Maxine's way of asking me whose side I was on. She believed they were guilty from the first second, while I left a small hole open for other possibilities.

"I don't think it's them." She nodded slowly, avoiding my eyes. We both stepped into the room and all eyes were on us.

The teenager was drinking water, silently eyeing Jessica. Jessica was looking at a picture of her family inside her wallet. Bradley was looking at the ceiling, probably counting the small mold stains.

"I have a very important question for all of you." I sat down, hoping this was the last time I had to interrogate these people. "Are you 100 per cent sure you do not recognise each other? And you are sure you only saw each other after waking up?" I made sure to look at all nine of their eyes. I wanted someone to confess this crime.

"I have no idea who this is," Bradley pointed his fat finger at the two ladies sitting next to him.

"Same," the teenager added.

"Jessica?" Maxine asked, staring right at Jessica.

"I want a lawyer," she replied, still sniffling, pushing back tears.

The whole room stilled. Maxine hummed in the back, daring me to speak. The teenager kept looking at her nails, inspecting them, paying no attention to Jessica. Bradley raised his eyebrows and looked toward me.

"Why do you want a lawyer, Jessica?" I whispered, creating a fake blanket of comfort for her. Maxine walked closer to Jessica and crouched next to where she sat. Even though she was crouching, Maxine's presence was so dominating she was more powerful this way.

"You know, only guilty people ask for lawyers. And I can swear you called yourself a victim a few hours ago." Maxine's smile was sinister realising she was right all along.

Meanwhile, I was trying to connect the dots in my head when another detective popped his head into the door. He whispered something into Maxine's ear and handed her a closed file. As she opened the file, I could see her mouth open slightly in surprise. I knew Maxine well enough to know something was wrong.

"We need to talk," Maxine whipped around. She grabbed my shoulder, squeezing slightly to alert me. I jumped out of my seat and followed Maxine outside. It amazed me how could one person create such a mess, not even knowing. We, as humans, should be logical creatures—but what Maxine said to me in the next few seconds, I couldn't simply believe it.

"We looked into Jessica. She's not just a mother of two beautiful children," she said, handing me a picture. I took the picture and the symbol she was holding on her poster.

"Christ," I swore under my breath. She was part of a small terrorist group—they first got famous for poisoning bigger farms that supplied big chain supermarkets. Seems like they upgraded their agenda from animals to people.

"She's been playing us. And what's worse, we have no idea of the extent of this small operation. God knows how many more were infected and how many are dead." Maxine cast a look towards the interrogation room.

"What do you think will break her? Her kids?"

"I'm sure that's just a cover. They are probably photoshopped together, and she most definitely has fake credentials. She played it well."

"So, why did she break her cover?" I didn't want to wonder. I didn't want to know. Her cover was blown, so she must've gotten a suicide mission note. But how? Who told her?

"It's one of them too." Maxine rubbed her temples and swore violently. I banged my fist on the table.

"They've been playing us, Winston."

"We got played hard." I hated being wrong—I hated the fact that I thought they were innocent.

"I had the lab run some more tests." Maxine threw a file down on my lap.

"You asked me why they would run a bio drug on some random people; turns out they're not so random anymore. The teen has been working three jobs to cover her mom's loans. The farmer is slowly losing his farm because he's running out of money." Maxine nodded towards the tax records I was holding in my hands.

"So what went wrong? Why did they leave Jessica to take the blame?" I asked.

"I think she had no idea it would go this wrong. Jessica has almost $200,000 in debt too. I think she was the bait. We spent the whole day focusing on her being involved closely with the operation, but maybe, after all, she had no idea what she was getting into." I rested my head on the wall as Maxine continued. My vision was blurry—either from the anger or from the confusion.

"So how do we find the people? Jessica won't say jackshit without a deal and I don't want to give her one." Most people who grabbed a deal ended up behind bars anyway.

"We don't. We wait for them to meet up with her..." Maxine couldn't continue because I spoke right over her.

"You want to let her go? Are you *crazy*?" I was close to breaking. No matter how angry I was, I had to hold my composition for my and her sake. Seeing me angry would scare her away.

"Yes. It's logical, and it's a good plan. We can follow her all day, or all week. We will keep them all close. The ticking bomb has to go off, Winston." Maxine grabbed my coffee mug and took a long gulp. She frowned at the end—black coffee without milk wasn't her favourite, but it's what got me through most of these long nights.

"We haven't seen any activity in almost 48 hours, Max. Just say you were wrong." I rolled my eyes and bit into my stale pastry.

"Shut up Winston. Your plan was more shit," she hissed out, holding a pair of ultra-red binoculars. We could see every move Jessica made. Every time she bit her fingertips or massaged her temples or checked the clock—we could see her.

In just a few seconds, we were jumping out of the car, grabbing our guns and charging inside. During our small argument, two men came into the building's lobby and paralysed the doorman.

Maxine ran through the doors without looking back. Entering the small apartment lobby, I saw them. Two older men, who looked old enough to be my age, were trying to call the elevator from the higher floors. Once they saw me, the charged at me. Maxine tripped one up, while the other managed to land one punch square in my jaw. They stood no chance against Maxine's quick movements and my lethal punches.

These men were no ordinary terrorists. After processing them, we found more cases in which they were involved. No matter how many biological weapons they tested, each one was worse than the last. They went from animals to humans.

"We found victim number four." Maxine barged into my office and quickly ran down the corridor to the morgue.

Four? But only three people were the suspects.

I ran after Maxine as fast as my legs allowed me.

"Explain," I rasped.

"The blood underneath their fingertips is from a man. A Colombian immigrant. That's why he didn't show up in our system. He was found dead in the river, washed up a few miles away from the cornfield. We found parts of him...his head is still missing. An expert thinks this might've been done while they were on the drugs." Maxine handed me a picture—torn limbs, blood, and burns were visible on what I think was someone's thigh. Or whatever was left of it.

"Do we need a confession?" I asked Maxine while gulping down the bile that was rising in my throat. Most things didn't even make me flinch, but this? This made me want to gag.

"We found all three sets of DNA's at the crime scene. They were under the influence of drugs, so there's no chance they could've done this on purpose. Can't say the same for the two men sitting in the interrogation rooms." She took the picture away from me and closed the folder, handing it to the secretary passing us.

"Sometimes, I wonder who could do such a thing," I pondered, while Max raised her eyebrows and lowered her head slightly.

"You were right," I concluded.

"I wish I wasn't now." She rubbed my shoulder and went away, talking to some detective.

The next morning, I was swarmed with hundreds of people—mainly journalists—who wanted statements and pictures of me. When something major hits this small news, they tend to go crazy over who gets the first interview.

But as I looked up, almost falling because someone stepped on my feet, I saw Maxine holding a file in her hand, ushering me to come inside.

And at that moment, I felt that everything would be alright again.

Chapter 8
Writer in the Light

Writer in the Light
26 May 2009

Manhattan, New York

It wasn't an everyday occurrence that a case this interesting hit my table. Four murders happened in the same town; all killed in different ways. I usually didn't work open cases, but my chief requested me specifically. Looking over the files, I saw all the bloody bodies—one was killed with a bullet to the back of his head, classic mafia style. The others were all killed with a knife or something sharp and small that left barely noticeable stab wounds.

I gathered my gun, tucked it into my waistband, and finally, after a couple of hours, left my office. I liked to be undisturbed, so I usually locked my door and pulled down my blinds. I walked up the stairs to another floor and my eyes zeroed in on Maxine, sitting right in front of Chief Kalman's door.

"Trouble again?" I had known Maxine for almost five years. She was a good person, but ruthless while investigating which led to her spending most of her time on probation. I think that's why we fit together almost perfectly—she was a carbon copy of the younger me, in a woman's version.

"Nah, I knew you would come. I also got the file. It doesn't look so pretty, does it?" After a while of tailing me, Maxine also got pulled into my 'dad' jokes. She had a copy of the same file sitting in her lap. It was closed, which told me she already had a look inside.

Our working relationship was simple. Although we were partners daily, we enjoyed each other's time. I even remember the first time I worked on a case with Maxine—how far she came from the beginning and how much more confident she was now.

"A penny for your thoughts?" Maxine asked. I sat down next to her on the old couch, trying not to sit directly on one of the freshest stains. The police department was severely underfunded by the state. The worn-out couch wasn't the worst—my door was so old and thin that you could hear me breathing through the wood.

"It's the same town but different methods, timing, and motive," I answered truthfully. Maxine was one of the only people I seemed to trust with my opinions these days. Most of my other colleagues thought I only took unattainable cases to boost my ego. They weren't that wrong.

Before I could continue to explain my reasons to Maxine, the heavy door swung over, and a short man with a stubble came out.

"Ah, Winston. Maxine, come in." He motioned for her to follow him. Chief Kalman was in his late 50s, and he had been my mentor for a long time. He was the one who pulled me up from the bottom.

"What now? Did you set the bank on fire? Crashed a car? Or maybe perhaps you're both taking a vacation, thank god!" He sarcastically poked at us and sat down behind his mahogany table. Chief Kalman had received so many awards for his brave heroism, you'd think he was charismatic and charming, but the old man was the exact opposite.

"Sadly, no vacation. We don't think this case is a serial killer—and we don't do normal cases." He acknowledged Maxine but gave me a stare. Maxine seemed not to mind, but we all know that it was only because her mom married Kalman years ago.

"Maxine, Maxine. This case is much deeper than any other case that you will find in that cold archive. I'm sure Winston memorised all those boxes at this point, didn't you?" He elaborated. Maxine rolled her eyes but looked at me for an answer. She hated it when I kept something to myself about a case. I could see why—it left her in a position where she had to act surprised when all she wanted to do was open her mouth to shout at me.

"He's not back, Mark. It's been almost a decade," I denied.

"Yes, he is. It's the Book Keeper, it's written right there," he grumbled, pointing to the crime scene photos.

The Book Keeper was not just any random psycho. He, presumably a man, killed his victims the exact way as was written in novels. Some old, some new, but all of them were done between October and January, each year coming back more brutal and with more dead bodies. Every state in America was scared. Even Hawaii at some point had a murder scare, but it turned out to be a false alarm. The Book Keeper was then turned into a book, a movie and so many interviews of family members that at some point, people got fed up hearing about it and finally forgot.

"Seems like he doesn't want people to forget about him." Maxine raised her eyebrows at Kalman's remark but I stayed quiet, reactionless. I was deep in thought, thinking about how old the Book Keeper would be today. Almost 60, based on the profile FBI provided us with.

I was not a cop yet when he went on his killing sprees, but even back then, I knew what I wanted to do. His signature was leaving a book from which the killing was inspired on the victim's head, covering their face. He left notes, explaining how the victim wasn't important in this case, but the novel was. Many tried to understand, but at the end of the day, it takes a psycho to understand one.

"Can't be him. He would be 60 at this point," I concluded and got ready to leave Kalman's office when Maxine spoke up.

"I don't think it's a man after all." She laid the case file on the table and crossed her hands in front of her.

Not this again.

"Max, not again," Kalman snapped. Although I hated to hear Maxine's version of the feminist talk, I nodded at her to keep talking. What I enjoyed most was annoying the chief, and this was the perfect way how to do that.

"Think about it. When men murder, it's only three possible motives—money, sex, or revenge. None of these murders have any sexual assaults, no stolen property or drained accounts, and the victims have nothing in common that could tie them to one enemy," Maxine stated. She rose from her chair and came to the board and grabbed a marker.

"You men always think the same," she grumbled and started writing names and circling them. "Instead of guessing who did it, which would inevitably lead you nowhere, let's focus on who is the author of these books, and let's find out any crazy fans. One of them must be the killer. Oh, and call Doctor Carrie Jones. She will help," she insisted, turning her back on me. I swore under my breath and it was now my turn to roll my eyes.

Doctor Carrie Jones-Heller was an excellent psychologist who assisted us with some cases a few years back. She won numerous medical awards for bringing new interrogation methods to us but preferred to lock herself with psychiatric patients who needed more help than the police force. She is also my ex-wife.

"No way." I put my hand up. I couldn't face my ex-wife again. We would probably kill each other in the process.

"Yes, way." Maxine grinned. This must be my punishment for eating the last part of her sandwich a week ago. We stared at each other and Maxine narrowed her eyes at me, but I blinked first. I threw my hands up to protest, but Kalman shut me up with a warning finger in the air.

"Stop being a child, Winston. Call Carrie. Get whoever you need. This time, catch him," Kalman concluded and ushered us out of his office.

"Did you have to bring her up?" I groaned, running my hand through my hair. We were having lunch, the Indian takeaway boxes scrambled on my desk. Maxine had her feet raised on my coffee table and I was sitting behind the desk in my office. We usually holed up here so no one would bother us while we discussed different points of view on our current cases. Sometimes, all I needed to crack open a case was a woman's point of view—sadly, I wasn't gifted such skill to pay attention to detail. I liked to assume things—I liked to daydream about all the scenarios, while Max looked for hard proof.

"Yes, Winston. You're both old enough to cooperate on this case, and I think her insight will help us. It's not like you must marry her again. Stop fussing like a baby." Maxine's Swedish accent peaked through her perfect English accent.

"I don't even want to see her." I rolled my eyes and put down the box stamped with 'Raj's place' on it. His butter chicken and garlic naan were the best in the whole wide New York.

"You know, you never told me what happened between you two," Maxine pushed and wriggled her eyebrows. She had been trying to crack me about my imperfect marriages for almost a year now. And the truth was I didn't want to remember what happened. Me and Carrie were married for only two years, which was a record time. We were in love, but our personalities clashed against each other, which resulted in many arguments and sleepless nights for both of us. Her family was nice enough to me, seeing as I was orphaned and often pitied by girlfriends.

Carrie was nurturing and honest, seemingly the perfect woman, but she also had trauma of her own that she didn't want to share with me. I was fed up with living in an act, so I packed my bags and left. She served me divorce papers later that year. I haven't really seen her since that day. We sometimes were both present in a random meeting, but it didn't go beyond exchanging looks and nods of acknowledgement.

"Let's focus on the case. My marriages can wait." I swept the theme under the carpet, but Maxine's look told me that she wouldn't stop asking. She rested her case and we got back to brainstorming. I could see she was getting restless.

"The killer might be a man, but he is organised and doesn't leave any witnesses. He also takes a long time to pick out his victims. The original killer took ten days between each murder. This copycat takes 17. Might be someone else after all." Maxine gulped. She was flipping the pictures of the old cases, which were filled with gore and blood.

"I don't know." I looked at the new crime scene pictures and they were barbaric. Humans didn't look like actual people anymore. After working this job for almost a decade, I was sure the devil existed, and he walked the Earth right next to us.

Maxine's phone vibrated. She looked at the screen for a second and answered almost immediately. "Hi, Mom," she said, masking the worry in her voice. I knew Maxine better now, and this was her way of lying to her parents about her job description. "Yes, we are following a case. No, Mom, don't worry. Yes, I will take care of myself." She skilfully told her mom she was too busy to chat now, and ended her call, promising she would call when she got home. I looked at Maxine and smiled. She didn't.

"She is too worried," Maxine blurted. I can see that she felt guilty for taking that call, while I reassured her more than once that it was okay with me. I didn't mind.

"Parents do that. It's natural." I tried to lighten up the mood, and she smiled softly.

"Who is this? Which author wrote this?" Maxine asked, handing me a picture.

A man, in his early 60s, lying on the ground. He was posed, his hands resting on the pavement next to him. He had a book laid on his forehead; *The Lottery*, by Shirley Jackson. This victim seemed to be surrounded by stones, just like the book dictated. This was a tribute to Tessie Hutchinson's stoning. He held a small torn piece of paper in his hand with a black dot on it. It seemed he drew the paper and therefore lost the lottery.

"Shirley Jackson," I muttered, putting the picture face down. The crime scene looked so brutal that I needed a few minutes to stomach it.

"You know what I don't understand? Why these books?" She pointed to the whiteboard. "Why did he choose these? They might be famous, but they're not exactly bestsellers. They have pretty bland murders inside." She was tempted to continue but stopped herself, waiting if I agreed.

"Are there any connections between the books? Any numerical clues in the names or years they were published?" Maxine startled me as she quickly came closer to the whiteboard in my office—she started to write the numbers of the year the books came out. I started to spin around in my chair, not noticing what she was scribbling. I could just hear her pen make a screeching halt. "Oh, god." Her back slumped. She kept looking at the board, and then back at the file.

"What?" I stood up and came to stand next to her. I looked at the dates, but it made no sense in my mind. The years weren't organised, some were from the 50s, some from the 90s but no date made me halt like it made Maxine.

"Julius Dannmark was born in 1948. 1948 is the year *The Lottery* was published. The year of the victim's birth is the same as the year each book was published. It makes sense. This guy is crazier than we thought." She explained.

"It's almost perfect," I whispered. Maxine looked at me with a puzzled expression, but I didn't give her any answer. I looked at the board, searching for the oldest date.

"1945. The same year the original Book Keeper was thought to be born. Maxine, I think we might just have a lead." I smiled to myself. Another chance to put this bastard behind bars? Sign me up.

Before we followed up on the lead, we agreed to take a day off. Investigating is tiring, and we got closer than any of the other detectives.

When Maxine figured out the years' purpose, I became sure she was ready to be a detective, and maybe my partner.

I always hated being partnered up with squares, but Maxine proved that her brain wouldn't weigh me down—quite the opposite—it would help us to solve more and more cases.

Upon arriving home, I fed the stray cats that always came to my apartment's window and fed myself some leftovers. Looking outside, I could see New York's skyline's pink hue, melting in with the orange hue. The trees were finally green and people wore their colourful summer clothing. Everyone was generally happier, and the stack of cases on my desk at the beginning of the working week seemed to thin out each time. Serial killers love winter, because nothing can cover a body better than a thick layer of snow or ice.

I was almost on the brink of falling asleep, but the vibrations my work phone made on my nightstand made me groan into my pillow. I was so close to declining, but I saw

Maxine's name and her personal cell phone number and rethought my strategy.

"What?" I groggily said.

"Sorry to wake you, but we have another one." She disconnected the call as soon as she gave the message. I rubbed my forehead and had to remind myself why I took this job in the first place. A picture of my mother flashed before my eyes and I had to blink twice to rid myself of her smile. I rolled on my bed, almost falling from it, and stood up. I put on my jeans and the rest of my outfit that I fished from my laundry basket. Maxine would notice and offer to help me with ironing, but me being me, I swore I could manage.

The car ride was quick; I smoked one cigarette and crushed it under the sole of my shoe when I got out of the car. Maxine, as always, was waiting for me at the scene of the crime. Next to her was Kalman, visibly irritated, shouting at someone through the phone. I tensed. He never went to any crime scenes with us, so what is different this time?

I came closer, nodded at Kalman and he just stared at me. His eyes were glossed over, and when I came closer to the body, which was unrecognisable, I realised why. Next to the dead body was a gun and a badge—one of ours.

"Who's missing?" I looked over at Maxine, who was running her hands over the file with names—names of every officer who signed up for his shift today and who was patrolling in this area. It was Kalman's idea to let other officers patrol the town, trying to catch our Book Keeper before he struck again. But we were late.

"Died two hours ago, maybe less." Doctor Ashbery stopped next to me and shook his head. His morgue was filled with the Book Keeper's victims, so he knew best how delicate the situation was.

Turns out, the detective was new and young, which was sad. Sad enough that Kalman himself raised the black flag atop the precinct.

The investigation went on as usual. I and Maxine followed up on leads, barricaded ourselves down in my office, and kept talking about all the cases. We got four hours of sleep each night and came back as soon as we could.

Six weeks passed, and we had no new murder. We ran out of leads to follow, until a woman came crying to the precinct about her missing husband. I again felt hope about finding the Book Keeper, but her description of his routine seemed too simple to follow. Her husband, Joel, disappeared two weeks ago, which meant the Book Keeper was either bored of killing his victims, or kept one alive for too long.

"Ma'am, could you tell me if your husband had any reasons to disappear?" I watched Maxine hand the crying woman another tissue through the one-way glass.

"You don't think he just disappeared, do you?" She sniffled again. "I love my husband and he loves me. This is not some young couple, Detective. We have been married for 30 years…almost," she stammered.

Maxine looked back at the glass, shaking her head. She gave the woman the whole tissue box and left the room, almost running into me.

"Winston, who the hell is this?" She scoffed, running a hand through her auburn hair. "We agreed to lose the dead-end leads, didn't we? So please, tell this woman her husband is a pig and let her go home." She turned around and walked in the opposite direction towards her desk.

I knew Maxine was right, but deep down, my mind told me this wasn't a coincidence. So, before I let the woman go, I took her husband's picture and her number. Walking up to Maxine, I came to apologise and invite her to brainstorm with me for the last time, but before I could say one word, Kalman shouted from the balcony. He shouted both of our names and ran down the stairs—I don't think I'd ever seen him treat something so urgently.

"Get your asses to the crime scene. There is a cop waiting for you, and you need to listen to what he has to say, ASAP. And Winston, bring the bastard home," Kalman dictated, and I nodded my head, grabbing my keys and rushing Maxine.

Now, you might wonder, how did we catch the Book Keeper? The truth is I don't think we did.

We arrived at the newest crime scene, which was swarming with news vans and other photographers, trying to snap a picture of the brutal state the body was left in. Pretty inhumane, if you ask me, but that's news. We walked in, but not before we were swarmed with hundreds of people asking questions. Other cops saw us struggling to walk through the crowd, so they came in and helped to keep people away from us.

A tall man in a cop's uniform came towards us. "Winston and Johannes?" We both nodded and he led us further into the building, which looked old and abandoned. "This was found in the hand of the deceased." He handed us a crumpled note and Maxine snatched it before I could. She unfolded it and rotated it so she could read the text, but she was quiet.

"What is it?" I peeked over her shoulder, and a chill ran up my spine.

Come find me, if you dare.

Maxine looked up at me, and for a second, I did not move, but then I ran to the closest computer and typed in the coordinates. They were in New York, not that far from us. "Let's go." I nodded at the detective and ran to my car. I could hear Maxine's shoe scuffle behind me, trying to keep up with my pace. I sat in my car, punched the gas pedal and Maxine's head collided with the headrest.

"Don't kill me, psycho," she groaned, but I tuned her out completely. I was too focused on getting a man behind bars tonight. I flew through all the red lights, not bothering to stop or even slow down. We were closing in when I told Maxine to open the small bag I had between her feet. I always kept my spare gun in there. Maxine wasn't done with her weapons training this year, but I hoped she would have my back. "Thanks," she whispered after loading the gun and resting it in her lap.

We were too close to back out. I opened my car's door after I braked too harshly, but Maxine was prepared now.

"Behind me," I reprimanded her and she clicked her tongue at me, probably rolling her eyes—I was too busy watching out for our killer to notice.

We entered the port, and hundreds of containers were present, all in different lines and colours. One was slightly cracked open, not too far away from where I stood now.

I could hear SWAT cars pulling up behind us, but I didn't wait—I wasn't going to let anyone else lock this bastard away.

I motioned for Maxine to open the container's door wider, and I had my finger on the trigger, ready to shoot. We barged in, and there was a man sleeping on a chair. Was he trying to laugh at us? His snoring made Maxine's face scrunch and shake my head. Maxine came closer, while I still held the trigger between my fingers and checked his pulse. Maybe this was just another dead body. Looking at him for a few seconds, it clicked—this is the missing husband. Was he the murderer all along? If so, why did the wife come to us?

"He's alive," Maxine whispered and I was surprised.

She hesitantly looked between me and the man, trying to figure out what I was thinking. A SWAT member also came in and patted me on my back, signalling we had support from the back. Maxine came closer to me while the container was getting full with the men from SWAT who restrained the man. Maxine's hand gently lowered my loaded gun and turned me around to leave. I was speechless—was this too easy? Or did my head collapse again?

I don't remember what happened for the next few minutes. I remember Kalman giving me a side hug and praising me, looking so happy again.

Maxine drove us back to the station and I even got to see how the now conscious man kept screaming 'It's not me' as they walked him into an interrogation room.

"You good?" Maxine asked me as she saw I kept staring into the empty space where they dragged the man. Our killer. "You got him. You won," Maxine said proudly.

"Yeah, I think I did," I mumbled, unsure. And I was right.

Not even a week later, a box arrived in the mail to the precinct, addressed to me and Maxine. A detective I didn't recognise handed it to me and I brought it up the stairs into my new office, which I now shared with my partner,

Johanssen. She was organising documents when I came in. I laid the package on her desk and finally got her attention.

"What's this?" She asked as I opened the cardboard box.

We both took a peek inside the cardboard box.

"Oh god!" She exclaimed, full of disgust when she saw the box's contents.

"Christ," I hissed.

A human head, its eyes carved out, with a book next to it. I was right. We weren't even close to catching the Book Keeper.

Chapter 9
3

14 November 2010

"How can you always win?" I fumed at Maxine, who just smiled. We were in our fourth round of chess, and while I was complaining about losing, Maxine was putting the clock into her bag. I was a sore loser when it came to Maxine and chess.

"Sometimes you have to lose, Winston," she said, and a flashback of a memory with my mother resurfaced in my mind. I smiled, remembering how much Maxine resembled her. Her wild nature, her jokes, and her smile.

Both of our phones vibrated at the same time. Maxine pursed her lips into a thin line and I took my phone, looking at the screen. It was the station.

"This is Detective Winston," I said as Maxine answered her call. I was sure it was another murder. Maxine looked at me with eyes full of worry—the last case hit me harder than we both anticipated.

Turns out, the Book Keeper was still out and we couldn't find him. Yet, Maxine's voice rang in my head.

After the last case, I fell back into my usual drinking game with a few buddies. It wasn't until a week later that Maxine had to slap me awake and shout at me for smelling Gin on my breath.

I guess that really woke me up from the state I was in.

"Case?" Maxine asked me. She raised her eyebrows after I didn't reply. I was still on edge about opening any cold cases so we've been helping around with other cases. "Are you ready, Winston?" She moved closer to me, laying a hand on my shoulder.

"As always, partner." I nodded and grabbed her tote bag to carry.

We both walked out of the park, unaware of who was playing chess two tables behind us. The station wasn't too far, and we made it on time. I nodded at the receptionist, who I took out last week—she was nice, but a little too bland for my liking. Seems like the universe was telling me to stop baiting women after my fourth divorce. "Chief Kalman." I shook the chief's hand, and he hugged Maxine.

"I'm sorry to be calling on your vacation days, Winston, but I'm unsure about a case that was handed to us," he said his voice taut. We both shook our heads and he led us to his office. Chief Kalman was a stranger to me until the last case—then he surprised me with beer one evening and he opened up about wanting to retire soon, asking me to take over his position. I declined, but he still persistently wrote me emails about it on my personal account.

"We had two murders—two strikes—in the last week. I contacted the FBI and they said someone very familiar got on their watch list in two other towns in two other states." He gulped his coffee. "They think he's serial. Last night he showed his face in one of the video recordings from the store where he killed his sixth victim." Me and Maxine were handed a thin file.

I opened it and on the first page was a picture of a man in his 40s, standing a bit pudgy and bald.

This is a serial killer?

I and Maxine were used to looking at men who spent half of their lives in jail, who were convicted of things like rape and murder—not married men with kids.

His file said he was happily married for over 10 years, had three kids and a dog, and more confusingly—he didn't even have a parking ticket on his file. This man was clean as a whistle, so why the sudden serial killer mania?

"He seems clean," Maxine quietly stated, only for me to hear. I shared with her Kalman's plans of leaving, and she immediately had to call her mother, Kalman's second wife. After that, Kalman had a scowl on his face every time he looked at me for almost a month. Maxine seemed to still be questionable about Kalman.

"Cap, are we sure this is him? He doesn't even have a parking ticket," I remarked.

Kalman raised his shoulders. "This is what the feds said. And the camera recording doesn't lie, Winston." Kalman sat down on his chair.

"Someone's mania cannot be dormant for 40 years, Captain. I think the camera was blurry and the feds need to sweep this under the carpet—the media is pressuring them, isn't it?" Maxine pushed. "Remember back in 1991, you arrested an innocent man and had him put on the chair? Almost killed him, if I recall correctly. And don't get me started on the Book Keeper." Maxine's snarky remarks made Kalman huff and shake his head.

"That's enough, kid," I cut her off before she could continue tormenting Kalman. Their relationship was strange, but I knew Maxine had authority issues. Sometimes they slipped while I was lecturing her.

"I'm just saying." She threw her hands up and crossed them.

"Winston, you know what happens when we catch the wrong guy."

Her words hit me right in my open wound. She was right, of course, she was. But I couldn't let my calm face slip in front of Kalman.

"Get out, Maxine," Kalman spoke up. I followed right behind her, ignoring Kalman talking to me. All he could see was my back now.

"Has anybody ever told you that you can be quite a bitch?" I remarked. She always did this when she was mad at me. Ignoring me, huffing, and puffing her chest out, and sometimes even rolling her eyes.

"Has anybody ever told you you're a shit detective?" Maxine prodded. I whipped my head to look at her—this behaviour was unusual.

"What the fuck?" I stammered.

"You pretend you're such a detective but you're slowly falling off the edge, Winston. Every case we cannot solve haunts you in your dreams, doesn't it? How many times did I tell you to start therapy? One day, you're going to become crazy," she muttered.

Spinning her chair away from me, she rapidly stood up and left me sitting at her desk. I wanted to forget her words and label them as her anger, but I couldn't.

That day, I brainstormed without Max. I couldn't think so straight after what she told me. Was I really falling apart? I mean, sure, it was in my family, but am I suddenly becoming more senile every day?

A knock on my door interrupted my thoughts. Looking through the peephole, I saw a head of auburn hair. *Maxine*, I thought. I opened the door and let her in, without speaking one word.

"I know you can't think like a woman. And for this case, I think you need a woman's perspective. So, I'm here. And I have notes," Maxine mumbled the last part, showing me her usual green notebook filled with everything—from her secret confessions to her crushes to crime scene pictures and scribbles of frogs.

"I'm sitting on the couch." I pointed her to my living room and walked right behind her to sit beside her.

"Want to hear my notes?" Maxine yawned, letting me know she was tired and didn't want to talk about our previous fight.

"Sure," I nodded, my voice laced with monotone.

"So, we know that our killer has very short periods between his killings. But his killing is very precise and he is very organised—that left me thinking, are these victims random?" Maxine closed her green notebook, and looked at me, waiting for an answer.

"They're not random?" I played into her script she must've prepared before coming over.

"They're not random. The ways he was killing were different but the motive was the same. He's angry."

"Enraged, I'd say," I added, and Maxine rolled her eyes.

"But that led me back to his life. He was happy, he was married, and he had kids, so why would he start to kill people?" Maxine argued. This was how we thought. We guessed, we argued, and we made a small mind map with unanswered. We'd drink old beer from my fridge and read jokes from Facebook.

"You think he's innocent?" I smirked, remembering how she fought me, swearing the man wasn't innocent.

"I think there needs to be some deeper meaning. You don't just wake up one day and become a mass murderer. You don't leave your picture-perfect family for no reason. Either his life is a scam or he's innocent—I won't accuse a good man of murder for god's sake," Maxine declared, standing up and rubbing her temples.

I was looking into my dead plant's pot. Deep in thought, I wondered if what Maxine said was true.

Can you kill someone without a reason? Can you become a serial killer overnight?

"Okay let's say he isn't the serial killer. Are we dealing with a hacker? How is he on the video from the gas station if he didn't kill that man that same night?" I whispered to myself, but Maxine must've heard it because she started talking about some new computer technology.

"Be quiet for a second, kid. I need to think," I grunted and closed my eyes after hearing her quiet down. I took in a deep breath and started thinking.

A man, a dead body. He was on the video, proving he was at the scene of the crime. But, at the same time, he was the perfect decoy. He had the perfect life—a wife and three kids, a stable job and no debt.

"Is there any way there are more killers?" I sceptically asked Maxine, who was standing in front of me, looking at me with a bored expression. She knew my ritual; she knew how I thought. My brain was switching from one scenario to the other, but one was stuck in my mind. *Was he the decoy?*

It already took us a whole day of theories and arguments in my thin-walled apartment to figure out that he might be innocent—maybe this is what the killer wanted all along—for us to think the man with a family was guilty of such a hate crime. I rapidly blinked my sudden headache away and looked right into Maxine's eyes.

"I need a fucking drink. I also need an IT guy who's going to dig up the dirtiest dirt on this picture-perfect bastard. And make it a double," I grunted at Maxine, who nodded at me and scrambled into my fridge. The last thing I heard was Maxine shouting into the phone.

In less than an hour, a scrawny IT guy with a Slavic accent rolled into my apartment with two laptops and his own Wi-Fi station.

I stared at Maxine who just shook her head and said; "Bran's the best. You wanted the best, didn't you?" She raised her eyebrows and at that moment, I was ready to grab my gun, which was currently scaring Bran off, and shoot him. I grabbed her arm and dragged her into the kitchen.

"I hate people in my apartment. I hardly tolerate you here, with your fancy-smelling candles and throw pillows. I don't want him to be here for long," I snarled at her. Maxine very well knew I was sensitive to random new people entering my apartment. Mostly for security, but a small part of me was worried some ghost from my past was going to catch up with me.

"Got it!" Shouted Bran from the living room. I and Maxine exchanged looks, mine showing defeat, her showing victory, and walked back into my living room again.

"Turns out Mr Picture Perfect isn't so perfect." Bran rotated his computer so that I and Maxine could see his screen. The brightness hurt my eyes, but I squinted and saw the page title, which said, 'Adoption Certificate.'

"He was adopted? How does that help us, Bran?" Maxine groaned running a hand through her hair.

"Maxine, my dear, get some glasses. Your suspect, Roy Mary, is one-third of a group of men." His Slavic accent was hard to understand, but Maxine's mouth opened a little and she gasped.

"He's a part of triplets, which means they all look pretty much the same. Let that poor man go, Maxine. I'm sure you tortured him enough." Bran closed his laptop and took a swig of his green tea, which had the words 'organic, vegan, and dairy free' tattooed on the bottle. I wondered how much that must've cost.

"Fuck. This is it, Winston. There are three of them. Six murders by two killers sound way more realistic than one killer." Maxine smiled and for the first time in a few weeks, I also smiled.

Not surprisingly, I couldn't even close my eyes for a consecutive minute—words like 'motive', 'murderer', 'why'? and 'planned'? kept repeating themselves in my brain. I couldn't sleep anyway, so I planted my hands next to my sides and lifted myself off the bed. Maybe I needed to visit the gym again—or perhaps call one of my ex-wives to cheer me up. It was too late for both things.

Calling Max was better than calling all or any of my ex-wives. She offered clarity instead of divorce papers. I lifted my phone to my ear and reached for my usual SOS pack of cigarettes which I resisted most days, but not today. I lit one up while I started regretting my choice to call Maxine.

"What the fuck?" Came from the other end of the phone. What Maxine valued more than our friendship was her beauty sleep. She needed at least eight hours per day, ten on weekends—I knew, because she stayed over most days of the week when we were on cases.

"Hey, kid. I need a buddy to brainstorm the case. You up for that?" I blew out the smoke I didn't inhale. Maxine strongly disapproved of drinking and smoking. She kept blabbing about how it's 'literal self-harm if you think about it'. She probably heard me blow out the smoke and I could hear her ripping the covers off herself and someone grunting behind her—perhaps another helpless man she saved from falling into a spiral of self-hatred. Maxine liked her men like that—struggling and in immediate need of some help and solid advice.

"I hate you. Unlock your front door," she mumbled, yawning before she ended our brief call. I loved that I could count on Maxine anytime to come and help me.

Meanwhile, I walked into my bathroom connected to my room, which was messier than my whole apartment altogether. One day, Maxine will have a field trip here and organise every single drawer I have with her clear organisers. Sometimes I wondered if she was sick in that smart head, but then I remembered I'd rather not know. I wheeled out my whiteboard which I scored from an abandoned high school where kids used to do meth. It was my very favourite thing about my apartment.

I heard my front door open and close and before I drew up my gun, I remembered it was Maxine. I kept writing; the heavy footsteps were definitely not Maxine's.

"Winston," a voice startled me. I almost shat myself.

"Christ, Mark. I almost died." I turned around and saw Chief Kalman standing there. I was almost going to crack a joke, but I saw the heavy blue eye bags under his eyes.

"Maxine's on the way."

"I know," he replied. I was unsure why my chief was here—was Kalman in trouble? Was he going through another divorce?

"I need to *leave*, Winston. I can't keep your secret anymore. I can't look at the photos or the evidence, and I cannot see your face every day knowing what happened there," he confessed. I shook my head.

"Kalman, I know you are a good man. And you know I'm the best guy in the whole force. You cannot open your mouth now," I urged him, imagining the consequences this will have on the force and me.

"Maxine will come any second, I think you should go," I murmured while I rubbed his shoulder and softly guided him through the door outside. I saw Maxine running up the staircase, and she stopped dead in her tracks when she saw me and Kalman in his state leaving my apartment.

Surprisingly, she kept quiet and continued walking. I was immediately alarmed and as I was opening my apartment complex's front door, I turned to Kalman. "If you tell her, it will kill her," I warned him.

"I'm very well aware. Solve this case and I can leave in peace," he vowed and turned his back to me—something he had never done before.

I walked back inside, tuning out all the thoughts regarding Chief Kalman, I continued my evening as I planned.

"I think one of the killing twins is dominant and the other submissive." While I was gone for less than five minutes, Maxine managed to fill my whole whiteboard with ideas and questions. In red ink were written questions, in green were things we knew and blue was left for theories regarding motive and emotional involvement.

"Why do you think that?" I slumped down on my couch. As a good mentor, I had to make her think hard. When Maxine thought hard, she was unstoppable.

"Look at the stab wounds. The morgue confirmed one set of stabs was deeper—this is the dominant twin." She pointed to some scars on the newest body. "They hit all the internal organs and places which would make you bleed like a pig. Big veins and bigger organs like the heart and spleen. On the other hand," she pointed towards the smaller stab wounds distributed in random patterns all over the front part of our victim, "these are shallow and tell us that the killer has a lot less strength. This could mean he has a birth defect or that he is disabled." She closed to file to cover the bloody body.

"I don't think so. I mean, yes, he is a submissive, but I think he is getting stronger. See the first body? His stabs were much shallower than they are now. I think he's starting to enjoy it," I muttered, running a hand through my hair to free my eyes.

"I'm not sure how someone can enjoy this," Maxine confessed.

"I know. But they're angry and mad at the world. You heard what Bran said." Bran showed us more than just the adoption document. He showed us their transactions, their whole lives mapped up on his computer. We now knew they were adopted and separated, changed adoption families often, and were both troubled children. No family ever wanted them, not even their own. And the fact that they kept one of the triplets just made them angrier. They had a whole list of criminal offences on their files.

Mario, the third triplet was safe in protective custody at the department. There were two agents always guarding him.

"What's the worst way you can hurt someone?" Maxine wondered.

I thought for a second. "I don't think they want to hurt him—they don't want to kill him. They want him to suffer like they did. It's classic revenge," I explained. Maxine's eyes were on me, taking a drag from one of my cigarettes. I never saw her smoke before but thought she needed it just as much as I did. She closed her eyes for a while, enjoying the menthol taste of the cigarette. Her eyes suddenly opened.

"His family. They're going after his family." She jumped up and ran across the room to get her bag and tucked her gun in her pants. She was still wearing her police academy-themed pyjamas.

I looked at her with a surprised expression. She grabbed my arm and dragged me to my front door.

"Maxine…" I softly said to slow her down.

"I'll explain in the car. Please, I know I'm right." Maxine's eyes pleaded—like a child begging their parent for a sweet treat. And I obliged. I let her drag me to my car and she dictated Mario's address. She called the precinct, barked at them to send backup, and quickly checked her gun and loaded it.

"Explain," I said as I punched the key into the ignition.

"Think about it. Your brother is the reason you had to go through hell in foster care, had to be put into adoption, and overall have a pretty shitty life. They want to take something that will hurt him deeply. And the only thing he has that they don't is a family. He always had that and it drove them mad," Maxine explained to me.

It made sense. Every person wants something they cannot have—it's in our nature.

"So what? They will kill his whole family?" I swerved the car and Maxine held on to the door. I was breaking the speed limit by at least 50, my siren sounding as far as four blocks in radius.

"Fucking hell," Maxine muttered. "Yes. They will kill his wife and his kids and if we don't get there on time, they might be dead already." She sneered at me and I stepped on the gas pedal as if my life depended on it.

"Let's hope we're not," I said but Maxine ignored me. She kept looking at other cars to make sure we didn't crash. I flew past the red light on the crossroad, almost running a group of people over. I'm definitely going to be put on probation—and Maxine with me. Maybe we will finally take that delayed vacation.

We stopped right in front of Mario's apartment building and ran out of the car. I could already hear the sirens of my colleagues sent to help me but I couldn't wait. Maxine opened the door and I motioned for her to have my back. We leapt up the stairs, checking the numbers on doors, waiting for 36. When 36 came into our sights, we halted.

"Cover me," I whispered to Maxine. The sounds of brakes could be heard from outside the open hallway window. Maxine opened the unlocked door and I quietly entered the apartment's long and narrow hallway. When I whipped my body in the living room's direction, I saw it.

Three kids were tied to wooden chairs and the wife was crying on the couch.

"Drop it," I hissed at the two triplets. One was holding the gun and the other was panicking, his expression changing when he saw me. I swear I could see the panic in his eyes.

"One step and his brain will be on the walls," the dominant triplet barked at me. I could sense Maxine was close, ready to shoot.

"Grab the knife," the dominant twin shouted at the submissive man. I could see him trying to decide what he should do.

It was my time to speak now.

"If you grab that knife, you're going to die," I announced, with a wide smile on my face.

"Don't listen to him," the dominant one barked at him again.

"Has it always been like this? I wonder how much he controlled your life." I kept my gun trained on the dominant one, while only speaking to the submissive.

"We want revenge," he croaked. I could see him struggling between me and his brother's dominant personality.

"Fuck you. I'll do it myself." He cocked the gun, and before I could shoot him, a bullet already broke through his skull. He fell to his knees, and Maxine was standing there, smoke still coming from her gun.

"The Devil called; said he wanted his bitch back," she murmured to herself, and I had no idea she was religious—I guess she knew me better than I knew her.

The door banged open again and a swarm of agents and cops came inside. They cuffed the other triplet and I got close to the wife and freed her from the plastic zip restraints on her arms and legs. She ran towards her children who were being untied by Maxine. The mother got on her knees and hugged all three of her children.

"Thank god," she mumbled and Maxine softly giggled.

"It wasn't God. It was her." I pointed at Maxine and the woman rose and hugged Maxine.

Maxine seemed surprised as if she hadn't hugged in a while. The woman kept thanking her when her husband showed up on the door's arch and she once again ran and hugged him.

Maxine and I were writing our final reports on this case when Kalman announced he was going to be retiring. He said he was going to stay until the end of the year, but afterwards, someone was going to take over.

Everyone was surprised, but Maxine seemed to be awaiting his departure. She looked at me with sadness in her eyes as I clapped like the rest of the precinct. We would still be partners, but she would have mountains of paperwork to do before going into the field.

"Congratulations," I said to Kalman when I found him after the party downstairs. He shook my hand and as I got ready to leave him alone to talk to others, his words brought up an icy cold shiver.

"One day, your past will catch up with you. And you won't survive unscathed this time."

Chapter 10
Doctor XZ

Doctor XZ
11 July 2011

Scottsdale, Arizona

Sometimes, I wondered if every person who's done a bad thing would go to hell right after they die.

Was I also on my way?

Or maybe because I put so many people in jail, maybe someone up there would decide to keep me in paradise—but I deserved hell.

Sometimes, when I catch the 'bad guy' he turns out to be better than I am. And that was exactly the case of Mara Billow. Doctor Mara Billow worked at a smaller local prison in Arizona, where hordes of dead prison inmates had been found right next to the fence, buried properly in big black plastic bags.

Me and Maxine were called to the scene of the crime. We were invited by the local sheriff and their police department which was in the smallest building on the whole street.

Walking in, we sat down in the waiting room. Most of the detectives recognised us and stared. Their secretaries made us coffee and Maxine was distracted. This didn't happen very often, so I was waiting for her to share what troubled her with me, but she was as quiet as a mouse. From her body language, I could see she was deep in thought, so I left her to think for a while. Looking in front of me, I noticed my chair was shaking slightly.

"Kid." I put a hand over her knee to stop her from shaking it.

"Yeah?" She whipped her head at me and replied with a shaky voice.

I wanted to ask what was bothering her but a detective came to collect us to take us to the scene of the crime. We sat in the back of a police car and Maxine kept looking out of the window. I wondered what could've happened—I knew the time was approaching for the anniversary of her mother and Kalman. Her father left years ago, even before she moved to America, but Kalman and her mom were still present in the annual family pictures. Maybe she just needed someone to talk to, or perhaps a vacation.

Before I could start to pay attention to my surroundings, the car stopped and the detective looked at me through the mirror and said, "We're here." He had a thick accent, I guessed Alabama. He wore a golden wedding band on his right hand and a cross was tied to his rear-view mirror, with a small inscription that I couldn't read from such a distance.

All three of us got out of the car and we went through all the prison checks—take your belt off, put your gun in the bin, show me your badge—all of that.

Me and Maxine went through first, Maxine's camera kept sliding off her shoulder. I could see she was tense but again said nothing, thinking this wasn't the place she would like to talk about it.

Walking through prison was never *easy*. There were only two types of prisoners; ones who enjoyed their time here, and those who wished they stayed home that one night before their lives were sentenced away.

Looking around myself, I wondered which type I would be. Perhaps I would miss the fresh air outside or maybe I'd miss Maxine and the precinct.

Before I could ask how much longer it would take us to see the crime scene, we were already there. I saw the warden, the cops, and the guards all standing in unison—hands in their pockets looking at a dead body.

"Detective Winston." The warden came closer to me and shook my hand. He ignored Maxine and touched my shoulder. "This isn't our first." He tapped his feet on the ground, signalling he was nervous.

"Same technique?" I scratched my stubble and felt Maxine crouch next to the body. In less than a minute, Warden Eisenhower told us the entire history of the murders.

He cleared his throat.

"It all started almost ten years ago. Back then, we all thought it was organised crime or a gang inside the prison—then bodies started to pile up in our small morgue. One day it was an inmate who raped a girl, and then it was a mass murderer from solitary. There is no connection between any victim. I swear we tried everything—their history outside the jail and inside, we questioned all inmates and nothing came up." He muttered.

All eyes were on him. I guess it wasn't usual for Eisenhower to open up about all the problems the prison had.

"We then started to officially investigate—but election season was up and our old governor wanted nothing to do with this because of his campaign. So, we contacted the FBI. They never even came to peek at the fucking dead bodies." He grunted and shook his head—I could see he was worried. Hell, if someone was mass murdering inside a prison that is filled with scum, even I'd be worried.

"We will try to help. But don't think I am promising that we will find whoever is doing this. There is still a very big chance it's someone from the inside." I nodded at Eisenhower and motioned for Maxine to speak up. She's been staring at me for a while, awaiting her turn to speak.

"Someone sliced the back of his head. I think he bled out, but not from that. The slice would hurt him; paralyse him even, but not enough to kill. His arms are bruised as if he was tied. I think this is personal," Maxine announced. I never doubted this woman, but today was different.

"It was personal, but this wasn't any friendly banter. This kill was impersonal. The killer didn't know the victim personally—they weren't friends or inmates." I turned to Warden Eisenhower.

"He was in a single room, usually kept to himself at lunch," he added.

"What did all the victims have in common?" I asked.

"Nothing."

"Come on, don't hold back information now. We're here to help, not to lock you down. I want to catch this son of a bitch as much as you do," I emphasised 'I'.

"They all targeted women and children in their crimes," he muttered quietly. I guessed he didn't want half of the prison whispering about how bad he is at his job—the truth is I didn't care.

"Explain," I maintained eye contact with Eisenhower.

"All of them either murdered women and children or raped them. All of them were doing time for violent crimes. We only noticed this pattern two weeks ago—Christ, you've been here for less than an hour and you realised. I'm so disappointed in how we proceeded," he criticised himself and cursed under his breath.

"So, either a woman who's seeking revenge or a man whose family has been hurt or killed and now sees other men as targets for revenge." I pointed out to Maxine who raised her eyebrows at me.

Eisenhower suddenly interrupted. "I don't think a woman could've done it, Detective. They're all big men and heavy as hell." His accent slipped through. "We also don't have any women in this prison—It's too dangerous. Not like any lady would sign up for this job."

"I think you should leave us to decide, Warden. I think we will need to have access to all personnel files as well as yours." I made known the fact that I was the boss now—even when the warden was around, I had an eerie feeling he was keeping things hidden from us.

Maxine stood up, towering over Eisenhower. I could already see how mad she was at him. His little misogynist speech about how a woman cannot take down a bigger man must've been meant for Maxine. I see he was around no women, so he probably had a small authority problem.

Warden Eisenhower nodded at me, completely ignoring Maxine. He turned on his heel and marched out of the room.

"How far mommy issues can go, right?" I smiled at Maxine, whose eyes were pitch black from anger. She gathered her camera and we left the room where the body slowly decomposed as well. I hated the smell with a burning passion. The flies and the fumes made me want to gag.

"Mother fucker," she whispered so only I could hear. "Who the fuck does he think he is?" She rolled her eyes and opened the door to a small space, which was previously used as a storage room, now turned into a small investigation room for us. She sat down on the couch and unbuttoned her jacket.

"Don't take him seriously, he's a bitch," I remarked. Eisenhower was a shit detective, and I'm sure he was even worse at his job.

"Please, he literally said women are weak to my face. I can't even look at his ugly face—and guess what, he's another misogynist? It's my lucky day." Maxine sighed and rubbed her temples.

"I'm saying forget him. We'll show him who is the boss." I winked at her and she scoffed with a smile on her face.

A while later—perhaps two coffees after our conversation—three boxes of files were delivered to our door by a fellow guard. And they were overflowing with files. Unorganised, dirty with stains and paper mites.

The people who worked at this prison were usual. They weren't math geniuses at 15 or didn't take any special college classes—some of them worked here for decades. Some of them had a criminal record for breaking and entering when they were younger. Everyone seemed average. All employees were sooner or later going to be cleared. No one had any death in their family caused by a man; no one was raped or assaulted by any man.

"I don't think the suspect is picking out their victims based on looks or nationality or race. I don't think this is victim projecting syndrome." Maxine shook her head and threw a couple of stacks of paper back into the filing boxes. "Half of these people are dead here, Winston. They're so normal that it hurts to even read their boring life stories."

Victim projection, as mentioned by Maxine is a syndrome that people involved in a crime as a witness usually get after years of trying to heal. They try to find peace and when they cannot, they start looking for revenge. Usually, these killers have the same victim preferences—seems like this one might be different.

"I agree. I don't think this is so personal that our victims know who hurt their families in the past. Maybe we should look at unsolved cases?" I questioned.

"I don't think so. I don't think this is fuelled by rage from not getting a clear result like someone would get in court. I think this suspect might be killing all these men just because he or she despises rapists. We had a handful of those." Maxine brought up more than ten cases that we dealt with which involved women with a vendetta against rapists.

"We should put together a profile." I nodded in agreement and wheeled out the whiteboard they brought us from the storage.

"Gimme something," I smirked at Maxine. I halved the board into two parts—one with Maxine's theories and one with mine.

"Woman, in her 30s, smart, works organised, and has a vendetta against violence against women." I wrote down what she said. Then I scooted my chair over to the other half and started writing; man, in his 40s, strong, manipulating towards other men, wife killed/raped.

"Why a man?" Maxine prodded. I didn't want her to know I also thought this was obviously a man's job—the strength would have to be immense to even pull this off.

"I think it's just one man with a lonely personality and a vendetta because someone hurt his wife, mother, or daughter." I raised my shoulders and nodded at her to question me again.

"What if, theoretically, it was a man and a woman? Someone inside this prison who works together—Batman and Robin's relationship. The big strong guy kills and the smaller one with the brain organises and plans. It makes logical sense." She shrugged, mimicking my bad posture.

I wheeled my chair closer to her sitting on the couch. It did make sense.

"Okay. Imagine; a woman manipulates a man, who's already in prison so why not help her? Maybe she's a lunch lady or someone who's supposed to be naturally submissive. She tells him her story about her vendetta about men and he agrees, pretending to be a good man for the first time in his life. She tells him about everyone here who raped or killed or even assaulted a woman and he kills them. Their relationship is symbiotic—he helps her to get rid of all the bad men here so she feels safe and she gives him the praise and manipulates him into thinking this is okay."

"A man whose wife was killed in a hit and run, or raped by a gang of men. He blends in perfectly as a cop or even the warden. He's been hiding this killing urge for years but now, he cannot stop killing. Maybe he's hallucinating about women like his wife who are thankful to him. A classical ego boost for this poor man." I bite my bottom lip in anticipation of what Maxine will say.

"Men aren't this organised and cops are even less." She gave me a knowing look. "And if he was a warden or a cop or even the parking lady, we would know if his wife was murdered or raped because it would be on the file. You lose, again." Maxine sipped her third or fourth coffee of the day. I wondered how she could live on caffeine for so long.

"Why do I always lose? My theory was good." I pointed a warning finger at Maxine and she spluttered on her coffee. She laughed, and we kept on writing our silly ideas on the board. Little did we know, we were standing on someone's dead body.

We didn't find out who was the killer for 19 days. We spent 19 days going through the files from the people who worked in the prison but found nothing. We interviewed everyone we could and yet again, nothing showed up. We were desperate, looking in small cabinets and laundry rooms for possible murder weapons.

We ended up *dry* every time.

I talked to the warden almost every day. His answers were getting shallower and vaguer every day. I'm sure he was pressured to close this case by his superiors, but I was here now, and no one was going to stop me from finding this son of a bitch.

After numerous arguments with Maxine, we finally constructed a profile of our suspect. We still couldn't agree if the dominant one was a man or a woman, so we left that category open for further inquiries. All the evidence was pointing to what we already established—a pair, a woman, and a man, or two men who were manipulating each other—one to kill and the other to think he has a chance at being good again.

For the time we were there, no new body showed up.

"You think they just stopped?" Maxine wondered, eating her salad silently. I wish I had an answer to that question, but I didn't.

"I think we're wrong about the profile. I keep thinking what if we're underestimating the power of one person?" Maxine huffed from annoyance to answer my question.

Truth is, this wouldn't be the first time we both underestimated the manipulating power of one person. In 2005, on one of our first cases together we were also manipulated by our suspects.

"I'm tired of this. I hate being here. It starts to smell like death in here." Maxine scrunched her face up. "What if the suspect and victim killed themselves? Maybe they felt us coming too close and decided it's not worth it." Maxine's breathing was slow and controlled.

"No. This suspect needs to be caught. They feel this overtaking urge to be the hero and prevent others from the same fate they suffered; in our case getting raped or molested by a man. They won't stop until they're the hero and all bad men are gone," I declared.

Maxine kept looking at the carpeted floor for a couple of seconds.

Then she gasped. "We were wrong," she muttered and turned to walk towards the board. She crossed a few words out; 'man', 'duo', and 'warden'.

"We kept looking at cases of molestation and rape—but what if our victim kept quiet about it? Did we ever check with the morgue about the slashes and stabs? What if she was trained?" Maxine opened the folder with the freshest murder pictures and looked up close at the slashes and stabs.

"An assassin?" I wondered. We never dealt with those before.

"No idiot. A doctor or a medic. Someone who knows how to make it hurt."

Maxine grabbed my arm and dragged me over to the east wing of the prison where most industrial rooms resided—laundry room, library, and the doctor's office.

She didn't bother knocking, just barged in without a second thought and I followed. The doctor sitting there was a man with grey hair, presumably 50 years old. We both exchanged a stare between each other.

"What are you doing here? This is the medical office," he challenged us.

"Who all work here? I need names." The doctor gulped and stayed quiet. Maxine wasted no time and started rummaging through the cabinets, creating a mess of important files and papers about the prisoners.

"Stop! Okay, I'll tell you." He threw his hands up and I could feel Maxine fuming. We were, close, I could feel it.

"I have an intern. Mara Billow—but she's a sweetheart! She wouldn't hurt a fly. She's been helping me for years," he began. Maxine snatched the file away from his hands and started reading between the lines, looking for what I presume was a clue—something that could tell us if Mara was the suspect we desperately needed.

"She's been working here for ten years?" Maxine pushed, putting her muddy boot on some of the discarded files, which used to be neatly organised.

"Yes, a little more than that. I swear it cannot be her," he pleaded.

"Where is she?" Maxine roared. Even I was surprised.

"She has therapy with some inmates, but that's on Tuesdays. She's not here today," he mumbled, heartbreakingly. He paused for a second. "Wait—she has one session with one inmate." The doctor started to scribble down a room number on a piece of small paper and Maxine grabbed it from his hand and brushed next to me on her way out.

"How did we miss the only woman working with all the inmates?" I cast a few looks towards Maxine, who was rushing down to the basement, where room 138 was located.

"You know why, Winston? It's because you're just like that warden. You don't believe us women have the balls to kill a man, and that men are always the killers—well, guess what? We can also be cold-blooded killers; we can run from you and you won't ever find us because you're prejudiced against believing in the power of women," Maxine grumbled and didn't spare me a look.

I didn't say one word after that; I just kept following Maxine—like I usually do.

On one side, she was right. I didn't believe a small woman could kill this many men but turns out I was overlooking evidence because I didn't want to think about the fact that even Maxine could be a killer.

But aren't we all? My brain prodded.

Mara Billow was locked in the basement. She and another inmate, Kevin Murdoch were chatting, as if this was any usual day. Maxine kept trying to kick down the door until Mara opened the door herself.

"Who are you?" She questioned.

"Mara Billow, you're under arrest for the murder of 11 men. You have the right to remain silent." Maxine cuffed Mara and we must've brought a lot of attention towards us because now, almost 30 men were standing next to us. Mara kept protesting and Maxine led her through the crowd. Men like me looked at her with two expressions; anger and sadness. Only if it was as easy as we thought.

Having Mara Billow in custody made us lose our attention. We didn't think there would be more bodies showing up.

The warden's dream was fulfilled—the FBI showed up with dozens of techs who searched the prison from the basement to the roof.

They found three more bodies. Two were buried behind the court and one's skeleton showed up on the scan in the same room we once resided in. I, Maxine, and a psychologist took turns questioning Mara Billow, but no one succeeded—she kept quiet, promising us she was innocent. We spent hours in that investigation room, but we had no real evidence. Nineteen hours after Mara Billow was admitted to custody, I received a phone call from the warden.

"I have three men who just killed themselves in their cells. They were all patients of Billow. I don't think this will end anytime soon."

I ended the call, not saying anything. Did Warden Eisenhower want me to apologise to him for getting the killer?

I was fed up.

I walked into the investigation room where I found Mara sitting with her legs crossed like a lady and a pack of opened cigarettes Maxine must've smoked already. Mara looked up but again said nothing.

I took another cigarette out of the pack and lit it.

"I assume you know about the three dead men in prison, right?" I questioned her casually. I wasn't like Maxine—I enjoyed the thrill of seeing my suspect's eyes widen with the realisation that I had them.

"That's sad," she hummed.

"But, it's your lucky day." I took another long drag. "We found numbers four and five before they could kill themselves—I mean, that was obviously the plan, wasn't it? If they kill themselves, there is no evidence tying you to the crimes, is there? But sadly, we found them. Alive and well, and number four is being interviewed by my colleague. He's singing like Billy Joel." I could see steam blowing from Mara's ears.

"See, the truth is you think you're smart. You think you're a genius. But I know you aren't. And what's worse, you trusted a greedy *man* with your secret—and he is very intrigued by getting famous for all the bad things you planned. Seems like you won't be getting your revenge anytime soon." I closed the folder of files and closed the open pack of cigarettes.

"What?" She breathed out. I have you now.

"You heard me," I whispered and blew the smoke out into the room. I could feel her hands shaking. Her world was falling apart.

"No!" She roared. "Don't let him take the credit for it. It was my plan. He is an idiot! He could never plan it like I did." She bared her teeth at me like a hungry wolf.

"Mara, Mara. You idiot," I chuckled and knocked on the one-way mirror window, which just turned clear. There,

Maxine was standing. She wasn't taking anyone's confession—she was here the whole time.

"You just got played." I tutted with my tongue. Maxine waved her hand at Mara slightly. I could feel how happy she was through the cement wall.

"Let me tell you something, love. Us men, we're the worst kind of them all." I smirked. Mara's eyes widened—and oh god, that felt so good. Seeing her trash around with her hands and knees cuffed like a prisoner made me smile to myself. A detective came to collect her to send her to the maximum-security jail.

The world lost one more killer today.

"How did you know there were more?" Maxine slurred, as I was helping her come upstairs to my apartment. The whole precinct was awaiting our arrival to celebrate us. Maxine came too close to the beer cabinet and mixed it with scotch and she couldn't walk properly now.

"I didn't. I trusted my gut." Maxine giggled and I dragged her inside of my apartment. Throwing her on the couch, I brought a bucket for her and took her boots off.

"What's your biggest secret, Winston?" She straightened up and almost threw up from the sudden movement.

"You'll know soon enough. Now sleep. We will probably have another case at my desk in the morning." I covered her with a blanket and went to sleep in my bed.

You'll know my secret *soon enough*.

Chapter 11
Criminal Cleaner

Criminal Cleaner
10 April 2014

Sometimes, you underestimate the people around you. It could be your family, your neighbours, or your co-workers. Your old doorman might turn into a psychopath, and your favourite Bodega owner turns into the head of a crime syndicate—honestly, how do we know people's true intentions? The truth is simple. We don't.

I was living in the heart of Manhattan for exactly 17 months. In these 17 months, I solved over 26 cases. I was on a case-solving roll—never meeting a case I couldn't solve. That was until we ran into the so-called 'Angel of Death'.

The Angel of Death killed six people in his whole killing career, which might not seem like a lot to most, but the way he did it, was almost artistic. Every single body was positioned differently, their eyes were always missing—we thought the Angel took them in as trophies. Back then, we had no idea he was laughing at us, mimicking our blindness, to the fact we couldn't catch him.

Experts from all around the world were called in to study the Angel of Death. He thrived off the audience and attention, always leaving us small clues. He was smart, and never left one hair or fingerprint on the scene. His usual motto was to break into his victim's home, strangle them with a fish line, and then carve them up. He used his scalpel the most, and always left it in his victim's hand. Each kill had a slight difference from the last one.

I was called only because I was famous for solving 'unsolvable' cases. Cases that sat cold in the archives, open cases that had no suspects—you name it. I was confident that I could solve this case like it wouldn't even be a hassle.

My confidence fell when I saw the first crime scene. I talked briefly to the policemen standing on the apartment's sidelines, mouths agape. The newest victim was even more cut up than the old ones. The techs said the victim was a man, but if you asked me, he could be anything. His nose and eyes were cut off, leaving only his mouth open. His mouth contained a small piece of paper, a clue of some sort. I came closer to the body when my assigned partner Russel startled me.

"I wouldn't go any closer if I were you. Death seems to follow those who come too near," he trailed off, whispering the last part.

"I'll be careful." I hesitated when coming close. The victim smelled of fresh blood, the tangy but metallic smell still evident. A technician was just grabbing the victim's wrist when I saw a small black smudge on it.

"Stop. Turn the wrist back," I stated, hand on the tech's shoulder. He slowly turned it around, and I swabbed it with a little cotton swab. Pushing it into a plastic bag, I sealed it and handed it to the woman whose shirt said, 'Scene cleaner.' She seemed like she knew where to put this, or who to give it to. I didn't even know her name, never seeing her before this.

I remember I went over the crime scene twice. I checked every drawer, checked every newspaper this man had at home, but no leads. Not even a hair. It looked like after our killer killed his victims, he mopped the floor. Not even the best techs could find a drop of blood on the floor or furniture.

This meant two things.

A, he killed them somewhere else and brought them here, or B, he waited for them to arrive home with a plastic sheet covering the whole apartment. It seems like neither of these findings is going to bring us closer to our killer.

I went home that night perplexed. I was currently living in this small apartment that had a bathroom, a small kitchen, and just enough space for one bed. I couldn't even fit my table inside this studio. I went to sleep, silently wishing for this case to be over already so I didn't have to stay here any longer than necessary.

The next morning, I was awakened by a loud ringing noise. "Winston speaking," I grumbled and pushed my head back into my pillow. Slowly opening my eyes, I saw the alarm clock say 7:28.

"He's done it again. I can't believe it," Russel agonised, and I was dressed in less than five minutes, running out of my apartment. Running to the metro, I pondered. The Angel usually took at least a week's break before killing again. That was his routine.

Routines are very important in the business of murder. Sometimes it happens that you can catch a killer based on their routine. You can catch them while they are in the middle of cutting up their next victim or pissing in their mother's apartment. Routines also give us a sense that our killer is planning another murder, which gives us time to try and catch him. But the Angel seems to be making sudden and rash decisions, which, if you are a murderer, do not end up positively for you.

"Give me something, anything," I grumbled, walking into the newest victim's apartment. Russel was already waiting inside, standing over the victim. He looked puzzled—his back hunched and sweat was covering his grey shirt.

"He's gone mad," Russel stated and turned to face me. "New body in less than 24 hours. His new personal record." I opened my small diary and started writing: Less than 24 hours, victim five, 13th floor. I desperately wanted to find a clue, something that would crack this case open. I felt hatred towards our killer—who kills two people in less than 24 hours and does it so perfectly? He must've been a professional, either a doctor or a cop. I scanned the room, looking at everyone's faces. I could see disgust, sadness, and on some, even boredom.

My head concentrated on the ticking of the clock. I closed my eyes and counted.

"Where's the clock?" I asked Russel who looked at me with a confused expression.

"If it bugs you, we can rip the batteries out." He mumbled as he looked at the body once again. I wasn't a fan of Russel—he seemed to admire each crime scene more than the last one.

I walked to the kitchen, then the living room, but I couldn't see it.

It did bug me; the sound of the ticking almost brought me to the edge.

Where is the fucking clock?

I closed my eyes and walked freely, listening to the sound of the clock which got more and more irritating. My eyes snapped open when I banged into the wall.

I couldn't find the clock, because it wasn't inside the apartment. I could hear the clock through the paper-thin walls. In my two days in this case, I never even thought about the walls of the apartment.

Another thing with murder in New York—there are people everywhere. Your neighbours, the doorman, and the damned people on the streets—you name it. There cannot be a scenario where someone wouldn't hear. I didn't bother telling Russel where I was going. I left the apartment and made a beeline towards the next one. I knocked but received no answer. I banged the side of my fist on the door when I heard a small 'I'm coming' from the other side. The door opened, and there she was. A woman, almost as tall as I was. Her whole body seemed hairless. From her bald head to no eyebrows—I looked behind her and saw a pudgy ginger cat waiting for her belly scratch.

"I'm Detective Winston; we are investigating a murder that happened next door. Did you hear anything last night?" I asked, while a tech walked behind me and said 'Hello' to the neighbour I was questioning.

"I know. I'm the crime scene cleaner. I was at the last one also. You said hi to me," she informed me.

"Oh," I replied.

"I also wasn't home last night. Had a date in the new restaurant down the street. Sorry to disappoint," she clarified.

"That's all right. I'm sorry." I seconded and turned on my heel to exit.

I felt like a complete fool.

Maybe you're losing it again. My mind echoed.

I was losing it again. I never felt so disappointed in myself while working on a case. This one seems to be full of clues I cannot understand yet.

The next morning, I feared there would be a new call, a new dead body.

But there wasn't.

I felt relieved and even rolled over to sleep for another hour.

When I awoke again, I was shaken. Someone was gripping my shoulders. I opened my eyes, and Russel was staring at me, muttering a small 'thank fucking god' under his breath.

"Good morning. What did you drink yesterday, you pig?" He shouted and I felt the urge to rub my eyes and wake up from this nightmare.

"What?" I croaked; my voice visibly hoarse. When I took a deep breath, I smelled the ominous, but usual, smell of blood.

"He's back." What?

"There is a dead body sitting in front of your door," he repeated. I guess I didn't hear him the first time. My head was banging.

Russel helped me get up from the bed and led me towards the group of people inside my tiny apartment. I rubbed my left eye and let him lead me, until he halted, and sucked in a breath.

A body, completely skinned sat opposite my door.

Good fucking morning.

"Who is it?"

"It's your neighbour. Seems like he was killed right after you left the crime scene. We have reasons to believe the killer is one of us." I hated hearing that. When the killer is someone you know or are close with, it's hard to find the reason or the motive.

"Bring everyone who was present at the last crime scene for questioning. I want to talk to everyone," I commanded while I came back inside my apartment, forgetting the 50 people who were looking at me like they were deer in headlights.

"All of you out!" I roared and watched them all scramble out of my small door. Nothing was keeping me sane anymore. I had the urge to throw everything out of the window.

My apartment building was old, and like most old apartment buildings had no camera systems or a doorman. That meant I was back to square one, only this time, three more bodies were haunting me. The next time I was leaving my apartment, I cast a double look in both directions, fearing I might be the next victim.

And just like yesterday, the technicians swept the entire floor of my apartment building, and woke up all the tenants in my building to ask questions, but no one saw anything. I felt hopeless. I, myself, went over to my apartment, searching for clues. Russel offered to make me a bed out of his couch, but I refused. If this bastard will show up to kill me, he can try. This shoe box didn't feel like my place anymore, so I took the liberty to sleep on my couch in the office.

Sleep didn't come easy that night—my mind was running with all the different possibilities of who it could be.

Most of the suspects were cleared by Russel, and others were given schedules for their interviews. I was kept away for the first few days of the interviews, but then I swore to Russel that I was okay. I even threatened him to let me in, and after a few minutes of bickering, he let me sit inside one investigation.

"Is this all?" I asked him after we left the last interrogation of the day. As tired as I was, I refused to go back home without at least one result or clue.

"Winston, we interviewed literally everyone. You have no more neighbours we don't know about. Here, take this home and dwell on it. Maybe this will give you a clue." Russel noted, as he thrust the paper into my hand and left. I rolled my eyes at his childish behaviour but opened and read the list nonetheless. I read every name, from A to X, and matched names with faces.

I closed my eyes and played the last two days like a movie. Every person I saw in my sight, I crossed off the list. Any faces I couldn't match were heavily described in my diary—including the infamous crime scene cleaner I met. I had seven people who we did not interview, and another four who I couldn't match to the existing name list. Three women, including her and eight men.

The next morning, I walked into the station with a smirk on my face—I was finally getting somewhere.

Walking into the cafeteria, I spotted Russel and made my way towards his table. He was gulping down his coffee and biting into a cold egg sandwich.

"I have 11 people who we didn't interview who were present at the crime scene. We need to go now." I rushed him, grabbing the sandwich out of his hand and running with it towards my car. I was putting on my seat belt when Russel came into my view.

The entire way to our first suspect's apartment, he babbled about how we were wasting time. "Maybe it's you," he reprimanded me. "You seem to love the fact that a serial killer is on his way to murder another victim," he asserted and I gasped.

"Look, Russel, you have this crazy problem-solver agenda, but you seem to be struggling every day," I elaborated and wanted to punch him. It seems I cannot win with Russel.

We interviewed four people that day before we got a call to come back to one of the Angel's first crime scenes. That worried me. Even Russel looked seemingly distressed. I was too busy focusing on the road to monitor his facial expressions.

I parked, and we got out slowly—as if we were both hyperaware of the fact that the Angel could have killed again, which would leave us even more lost than we were now. The cops greeted us silently while we walked on the second floor. "You're shivering," Russel pointed out and I took a deep breath in to steady myself.

We weren't met with a new dead body. We were met with something much worse.

"We found evidence, evidence that can be very…misleading." A cop prepared us for what we were about to witness.

"Is he killing again?" Russel asked.

"Take a look for yourself, Detective," the cop spat out. I was distressed.

Clicking the button, a grainy blue-hued video played. The timestamp was right around the predicted murder. For a few seconds, there was nothing. Only a couple of doors and some barking in the distance. But then—I was sure I was dreaming.

A man, around six feet tall entered the view. He had a jacket on, but at first, I couldn't make out the three words on it. The video was so low in quality that it seemed like I needed glasses to properly see what was happening.

The guy from IT made two clicks on his computer and the image took a little photo and he magically enhanced it so clearly, that I could make out the letters. They read: 'J. Russel.'

I was too afraid to look at Russel. Only two hours ago, he was accusing me of being a serial killer, and now, it seemed like the tables had turned.

A fellow cop came behind Russel, and I heard the sound of the metal cuffs clicking open.

"Detective Russel, you're being arrested for murder." And after that, it seemed like the whole world went blank.

I went back to the station, alone. I was too distressed to call someone. In my head, it made logical sense.

We interviewed everyone, except him. Everyone had an alibi, except him. He was the first to arrive at my apartment when I didn't answer my phone. But there was simply no motive. I wasn't allowed to question Russel, but I sure as hell was standing behind the window.

I weirdly felt…*betrayed.*

Maybe if I said yes to staying with him, I would've been dead already.

Yet it still doesn't make sense, does it? The question kept replaying in my head, as did the grainy video.

The Angel of Death's career was so short, and James Russel had been a cop for a long time. The tests would show he was a psychopath, sociopath—and people could see if there was something wrong with him.

But James was normal. He showed no signs of mania when I was around him for a couple of weeks. He had no wife, no family; he didn't even have a dog. Loneliness can make you go crazy, I guess. Not crazier than wondering if you would have been next if you slept on his couch.

James Russel was tried and sentenced very soon after the last time I saw him. The whole of New York wanted to see him in jail. I remember going up the stairs to the court and seeing thousands of people marching for the six deaths he caused. They held up signs, I quote 'maniac', or 'killer', or even 'kill this son of a bitch'.

A few weeks later, me and Jane, the crime scene cleaner met up for coffee. She said I would need a friend after going through all of that. I agreed because I needed someone to listen. Jane sat opposite me at the local bar. She still had a bald head and no eyebrows, but now instead of that, I was noticing how red her nails were.

"And I still can't believe it was him, you know?" We were four beers deep into a conversation, where I kept blabbering and she kept nodding her head. I felt my head getting heavier from all the alcohol I already consumed, but it didn't stop me from ordering two more shots—one for her and one for me.

After a few beats of silence, she spoke up, "I don't think he did it either." She offered me a small smile and gulped her beer.

"You don't?" I wasn't sure if I heard her correctly. The bar was now full of teenagers who didn't fail their finals or get into college.

"Listen, I don't think anyone can be that good at killing if you're not a professional," she blurted.

"Exactly!" I returned.

"It's too damn hard to be a good killer," I concurred.

"It's like the Angel of Death knew if she didn't leave any evidence, no one would ever find her. My plan was so brilliant, that no one even guessed it could've been me." She smiled, sipping on her beer.

My plan was so brilliant.
No one even guessed it could've been me.

"Did you just say 'my plan'?" I questioned her.

"Oh no, sorry, this beer is stronger than I thought. I meant his plan," she explained, but I felt a cold wave of sweat hit me. I was completely sober, my mind racing a thousand kilometres.

"Should we order another one?" Jane's voice startled me.

"Sure." I needed to know more. She raised her hand to signal to the waiter and I slumped down on my side of the booth.

Christ, how did I miss her?

Chapter 12
Guilty Widow

15 September 2019

September barely arrived when another case file hit my table. I had no intention of even opening it this evening, but the small note attached to the thick, worn-out file case changed my mind. The note was addressed to me from my old friend at the morgue, Doctor Ashbery. I and Ash go way back into the 90s when his wife got arrested for reckless driving and I was the only detective available at two in the morning. She was meek, not drunk, speeding home to catch her husband presumably cheating with his assistant. He showed up and she jumped into his arms, cheating assumptions already forgotten. And ever since then, we both found a mutual understanding.

That night, I and Ashbery silently shook hands and I was owed yet another favour. I cashed my favour back in 2006 when I needed to illegally find out the identity of my (stolen) case. He did the DNA test without questions, which was our friendship's presumed end. But here we are.

My eyes slowly read over the note, noticing a few words with grammatical mistakes. Ashbery was always writing scribbles—quick and carefree, never giving a damn about grammar or the twitch in his hands, which made his cursive crooked. He wrote, "This case is one of the worst I've ever seen. This one goes straight to hell."

This was Ashbery's way of warning me of the gruesome pictures I might see. I grabbed my coffee mug and took a sip of the still-hot coffee.

It burned my tongue slightly, but not more than the bile rising up my throat when I saw the pictures in the folder for the first time.

Opening the case file, it seemed no different than any other cases I'd handled before. A 29-year-old wife killed her husband, presumably because he cheated on her. The usual 'crazy-wife syndrome' was written all over the case.

I could just imagine it. The house was quiet, she walked around for a while, hoping her husband would be back before the sun set below their visible horizon. But he did not. Instead of returning home to his overly loyal wife, he spent his evening with her best friend, or perhaps even her mother. Mothers tend to be nasty when it comes to their daughters.

So, he came home, visibly drunk with red lipstick on his mouth, the type of red lipstick that screamed 'fuck me' not 'take me on a date', she got utterly mad and shot him in the middle of his forehead.

But that's not all. His eyes were missing, just an empty bloody socket looking straight at me. I couldn't imagine how much precision it would take to carve them out this perfectly. A small voice in my head questioned my initial suspect guess.

Ashbery was right; these pictures looked like someone just pulled them from the deepest depths of hell. My first thoughts were, confusingly, back on Ashbery.

Why would he send me such an easy case?

It was clear the woman killed her husband, and she deserved to be in jail. So why is this case file sitting on my desk?

I leaned back in my chair, closing my eyes for a second. Ashbery knows me—and he knows I don't take easy cases. I like a challenge, for better or worse. The kind of challenge where I cannot sleep for days until I solve this case.

So, I do my usual routine. I close the blinds; turn off the lights, lock my office door and lie down on my couch. I pop two small white pills into the palm of my hand, and I'm out like a baby in less than ten minutes. I, perhaps, should have made clear that I needed to visualise this case to solve it. The two small pills are Doxepin, a drug that makes insomniacs sleep.

No, I'm not *addicted*.

No, these aren't *mine*.

I borrowed them from a pimp I put in jail last week. They seem to be working well. These days, sleep comes harder to me than a good day.

I'm wide awake and self-aware in all my dreams. I imagine a woman, small and brunette, in a mid-century-styled house. She's sitting on a red couch, waiting—muttering 'God' under her breath every time she looks at the dainty watch on her wrist. She made him dinner, reheated it twice already, and she's ready to go lay down with her tired, but loving husband.

Scratch that.

She's a tall blonde. Scandinavian furniture fills the house, and the omniscient glow of the pool reflects on the white and cream walls of the small home. She isn't waiting on the couch like a loving wife. She's in the shed, looking through piles of boxes, until she finds the one labelled, 'Luke's toys.'

Luke is her husband, and this is his gun.

She never used a gun before, but it fits in her hand—It fits perfectly, like a missing piece of the puzzle she's been searching for. In her mind, she won already. She's waiting for his tyres to screech against the pavement in front of the house.

She is ready to kill.

Her Gone Girl fantasy is replaying in her head. He shows up at the door, and she fires the small gun.

Bang.

The shot sends out a loud noise. Her eyes are ringing and her vision is hazy.

She thinks she's smart, but she is not prepared to run away from his shaking body—she of course misses his heart and shoots him in the shoulder, seeing him fall to his knees and beg her, bleeding out slowly.

She cares, deep down.

She drops the gun to the carpet—stained with his blood seeping slowly out of his body—and kneels next to him.

The loving wife still loves her cheating husband.

She shall go to jail and mourn her crime while he will enjoy another young appealing woman who's not his wife. She even calls the cops, confessing all her crimes and sins, and telling the pigs exactly how she planned the unfinished job. They nod, giving her a glass of water.

This case is an easy one, so why is it on my desk and in my dreams?

I don't remember the ending of my dream, or if she's guilty or not. I simply sleep, letting my actual dreams play with my head. The next morning, I called my secretary Samantha into my office and had her call Doctor Ashbery.

Not even two hours later, he's here, wide awake in my office with a small coffee in his hand.

"Winston, long time no see," he greets me, wrapping his arm around my back. I can feel his cologne flush my nostrils—working in a morgue must be unappealing to his wife, so he masks the smell of his dream job by drenching himself in the cheapest perfume he could find in the small corner drugstore—classic Ashbery.

"Ash, what the hell is this case?" I cut right to the chase. I hated small talk, and what I hated even more was catching up while knowing that there was nothing to catch up on. Ashbery was going to retire soon and my cases weren't in his jurisdiction, so frankly, there was nothing to talk about.

"I knew her."

He paused for a second, looking at me for some form of reaction. I scoffed and closed the file, spinning my chair to face the wall.

I had one policy—I didn't take family cases, cases tied by friendship or partnerships. People are dishonest, they like to lie and make things up—it's in our nature.

"Winston, I hate this more than you do. But Jane," he took a deep breath, "she loved her husband so much; she would never have the heart to kill him. I don't believe in it, and looking at you, I think you don't believe in it either." Ashbery sat down on one of my office chairs, collecting dust in front of the whiteboard.

"Oh, fuck off. Why wouldn't she kill him? It's the usual scenario and you know it." I rolled my eyes at Ash and he cocked his head to the right side. He was challenging me.

"Then why am I here, Winston? I know you thought about it. It's the scenario, isn't it? So what doesn't make sense? Why didn't you throw this case out yet?" He concluded the truth.

There was something weird about this case.

"Let's say you're right. Let's pretend she didn't kill him. Who did then? He didn't show up in your morgue for no reason." I murmured.

"Look, Ash, you know me. I want to know if she killed her husband, but no prosecution or any evidence is pointing to the fact that she is innocent. I'm sorry." I shook my head when he opened his mouth to try and change my mind, but I had already made up mine. To further make a point, I stood up and took the file, stuffing it into my unsolved case drawer.

"You will solve this, Winston. I know you will," he said as he turned around, putting his coat on and grabbing his briefcase."Truth is I know you want to solve it more than I do." He smiled as he opened the door and left, letting the smell of his cheap perfume linger.

And hell, he was right.

The next morning, I called a cab to the Hillfort Sanatorium. A small building being renovated which didn't look like it housed the worst of the worst—from psychopaths who killed children to rapists, who were better off in the middle of a forest in New York, instead of a big commercial jail.

Pulling up to the curb of the sanatorium, I paid off my driver and opened the doors to the building swiftly. I was expecting a guard or a receptionist, but the building looked run-down. I rang the small bell on the counter, a visible layer of dust catching my attention.

"I'm coming!" A woman's voice broke me from my trance.

A woman indeed did appear. An older redhead, with a few grey strands in her hair, wearing a vintage worn-out nurse's uniform.

"Hello, and welcome to the Hillfort Sanatorium, how can I help you?" The nurse put on her biggest smile, and I heard a scream somewhere in the distance.

"I'm looking for Maura Jane Smith, she should be here. I'm Detective Winston." I flashed her my badge and she nodded, busy typing on her computer. I looked around, but the place was destroyed. Small cracks everywhere, the pipes were leaking, and there was un-mopped blood on the white tiles, filthy with dirt from all the years.

The nurse whipped her head up to look at me again, and I brought my attention back to her.

"Sir, I must warn you—Maura isn't a...nice girl. She's mean as hell." The nurse let her mid-western accent slip out as she finished her sentence.

"That's all right with me. I know what she did. I just need a few minutes." She nodded and pulled out a couple of stained papers for me to sign—the usual documents concerning my safety and the safety of the patient.

Not that I was the good guy with the mass murderer in a small room without a lock.

The nurse led me through the sanatorium to the end, where a small room without a door caught my attention.

A woman, Maura, sat inside, drawing with charcoal pencils, and whipped her head up to see us approaching.

"Maura, sweetie, you have a visitor," the nurse said with as much sugar coating as possible. Maura narrowed her eyes at me, but as soon as she saw the small gold flash of my badge she stilled.

"I won't say one word," she said, directing her words at me but still staring at the nurse.

"I just need you to nod, Maura," I said swiftly, as the nurse turned around to exit. But before she made her way to all the other patients, she stopped in her way and leaned closer to my ear.

"Don't tempt her," she whispered and looked at me for the last time, before closing the wooden door and leaving me in the room with my suspect.

"Didn't you hear that I'll be stuck here for the rest of my life? What else do you want?" Maura snarled and picked up her charcoal to paint again. She started making sudden, harsh lines on the canvas. I sat quietly for a second, wondering what to say.

In fact, she was right—no matter what I was going to say wouldn't take these few years of her life wasted in prison back, and neither is it going to bring back her husband.

"I want to know the truth, Maura. I have a friend who believes you are innocent." I leaned back into the wall and shuffled in my pocket to find a cigarette.

"The truth was decided a few years ago, wasn't it? No matter what I will tell you, you won't change the last few years. To be honest, I have no idea what day it is or the year. Time seems to stop here." She turned her head back to her canvas.

"Doctor Ashbery sent me here. He seems to think you're really innocent." I looked around her room, seeing the walls covered in her black oil paint and charcoal. Before, I was looking for fire sensors, but this godforsaken place has none.

She kept quiet. I could see she was surprised by hearing the name.

"Humour me. I'm only looking for the truth. You got nothing to lose, and neither do I." I raised my shoulders and lit my cigarette.

She made no movement of acknowledgement—only turned her head at the window and started speaking.

"I want one too. And tell me what date it is today." She sat down comfortably on her bed, putting the canvas down with the pain. I handed her one cigarette and my lighter, waiting to take it back.

"Don't worry, I only seem to kill cheaters, so you might be safe." She chuckled at her own joke, but I stayed silent.

"It's 21 September 2019. You've been here for a little over three years." I took a long drag from my cigarette and she seemed to do the same, mirroring me.

"I know you might hear this a lot, but I didn't kill my husband. Yes, I *wanted to*, but I didn't. I should've thought. Seems like destiny made the call for me."

She chuckled again. "My husband was a politician, you know. Men like him don't stay faithful for a long time." Another drag, another puff into the empty room. "I knew he was cheating—I knew he was going to cheat before I married him, but back then I believed I could change him. Women like me, that's all we want. One faithful husband, and yet mine was anything but. You know, sometimes I wonder what would my life look like if I never married him." She rubbed the side of her head, and I pulled out a small diary I had in my jacket. I opened it on the first page and crossed out the first sentence, which stated, 'Wife was dumb.' With a big D.

"So, you claim you didn't shoot your husband?" I asked, no emotion lacing my voice. At first, I completely forgot that I was in a room with a psychopath, but it started to crawl back into my mind, making the hairs on my back stand up. I dealt with worse, but it still scared me to look this woman in her eyes.

"I never held a gun in my hands. I am strictly against violence, believe it or not."

I obviously didn't.

"I know how I must seem—a crazy woman who swears she didn't kill her husband, but it wasn't me, detective. What motive would I even have?" Her eyes were pleading, but I had to stay silent.

"Prove to me that you didn't kill him, Maura Jane. Give me one piece of evidence, an alibi, or a friend's confession—give me something, otherwise, you will rot here forever. I'm your last chance, Maura. I know you think you're innocent, but the whole state thinks differently." I passed her another cigarette and swore I could see a small tear escape her eye.

"He owed money. My husband was a gambler, in secret of course. There was a bookie; his name was common, something like John, or Josh. He came one week before my husband's tragedy. I was home, alone, and he told me if I didn't have the money, that the boss was going to come and take me as payment. I didn't believe him—I still trusted my husband back then." She lit the cigarette and blew the smoke toward the ceiling. "I've been thinking…Maybe it was the people he owed money to. People like that have guns," she concluded.

"You also had a gun home." I shrugged. I wasn't buying this—A politician killed by the mafia isn't unheard of, but if he owed money, the money would come up on some documents.

"I had a gun, and I had a million dollars. Now I have neither and I'm locked away in a Sanatorium. Funny, isn't it?" She straightened up, and I had to replay her last sentence in my head.

"What money are you talking about? There was no money mentioned in the trial." I pulled out my notebook filled with the facts about the murder, but nothing said anything about money anywhere on the case file.

"After my husband died, and I was taken to jail, my mother wanted to bail me out. I told her to access the shared money in our account that was created after we got married. The account was drained, and as I remember, my husband always kept at least two million dollars on that account. When she called me in the jail and said the money was gone, I thought the police took it as evidence. Back then, it never occurred to me that someone could want them as payback. But now, it seems very likely." Maura folded her hands against her chest, and I had to take a deep breath.

"Who knows about the missing money?"

"No one. I had no explanation for it to my mother, so we just left it and took money from another account. The police never really paid much attention to what I was saying, anyway, so I assumed they took it. Perhaps my mother-in-law or someone from Luke's campaign took them to fund a charity or something." She shook her head, but mine was filled with possible scenarios of where the money could've gone.

"If the money wasn't stolen, or did not vanish, who would get it after Luke's death?" I had to ask, not biting my tongue.

"I signed a prenup. Not a cent would go towards my name. All the money, the houses, and the campaign would go back to his parents, and they have all the power over it. I think they're somewhere in the Caribbean, enjoying their son's fortune." She laughed dryly.

Does a parent kill their own child?

"How did his parents react to his death?" I scratched my beard and Maura Jane smiled.

"They had no idea until the police told them, but I'm sure they shed some tears for the press. Luke was an only child and you know how that works." I did know how that worked indeed. As an only child, the parents had nothing else to fret over than you, and therefore you were the only apple of their eye.

I waited for a minute.

"I think I have all I need, Maura. I promise I will investigate your case." I stood up, gathered my belongings, and turned around to leave.

"Don't rush. I have all the time in the world." Chuckling humourlessly, she grabbed her canvas and continued as if I had never shown up.

On my way back, I kept wondering if a parent could kill their own child. Luke was rich, but so was his family. So maybe money wasn't the motive in this case.

As soon as I closed the doors of my apartment, I opened my laptop and did some digging. 'For Family' was the name of the political campaign Luke was leading. His social media was clean, with only pictures of himself with his followers, some campaign pictures, and pictures of children in Africa, who were smiling into the camera.

I wondered how little it took for them to look happy. Some new toys or clean water perhaps.

His online presence was clean. I didn't find any incriminating pictures, gossip sites, or rumours. It seemed like this man was a walking saint.

I stopped myself from reading another positive article when I heard my phone ring and vibrate. Looking around, I saw it on my kitchen counter and answered.

"This is Detective Winston speaking; how can I help you?" I asked.

"Hello, Detective Winston," a woman's voice greeted me. She sounded like Maura, but her voice was high-pitched. "I heard you went to visit my daughter-in-law. I must remind you that she has signed an NDA to prohibit any false information from getting spread after my son's death. I now will contact your captain to silently close this investigation you have going on, as soon as possible. My son's killer is where she should be. Please do not contact Maura Jane ever again."

The line went dead after her last words—My suspicion was now proven correct.

Luke's parents knew what happened that night, yet for their image, they refused to acknowledge that they sent an innocent woman to jail for a crime she didn't commit. Dialling Ash, I had to light a cigarette to collect myself.

"Winston? It's almost midnight," Ash grumbled, his sleepy voice making me chuckle. I heard his wife complain from the other side of the bed. Shuffling, Ashbery stood up from his bed and navigated towards what I presumed was his office.

"The Devil doesn't sleep, does he?" I took a long drag out of my cigarette.

"You were right. It wasn't her. His parents were riding right behind the murderer. They know, but I'm taken off the case. Is there any way I can access any evidence that was found at the murder scene?" Even a grain of rice was going to cut it.

He sighted. "I left you three voicemails, Winston. I went to look for the box of evidence I kept in the archives, but it was gone. The entire box with all the evidence convicting Maura Jane is gone." I stilled. Fucking shit.

"The cameras?"

"Wiped, as if the cameras weren't ever there," Ashbery replied.

"Fucking hell." I wanted to throw my phone out of the window, but I refused to lose my calm demeanour in front of Ash.

I bid my goodbyes and ended the call.

Maura was going to rot in jail, and I couldn't do anything about it. Her story will never be solved—whether it was Luke's parents, the mafia or even Maura—I would never know.

I would stay up all night, sleepless, thinking how could have I let this happen.

Did I do enough?

Was my pathetic attempt at opening her case again enough?

I should've done more. I should've made more copies. I should have paid more attention to the parents.

It's too late, my mind reminded me.

I think the worst feeling that can follow you for the rest of your life is guilt. No matter how many cases I solved after Maura's, I could still feel the feeling of uneasiness at the back of my head.

Every time I saw a woman that resembled Maura, I thought about her.

I tried to visit her, but every time I showed up, she was 'occupied'. At some point, I stopped trying. I made up my mind, thinking she simply didn't want to see me.

Now almost two years later, I get a phone call, in the middle of the night.

The same old nurse from Hillfort called, and said, "She's gone, detective."

Turns out, Maura managed to break the mirror in the shared bathroom and she slit her wrists. She left no note, but I knew.

I knew this was the best thing that could've happened after her conviction.

Maura was free, but my mind was forever clouded with the guilt of not solving her case.

Chapter 13
Article

Detective Winston's Unresolved Case: A Tragic Tale of Consequences
Published by *The New York Times*

By: Levi Magnussen-Knowles

While Detective Winston may be celebrated for his achievements in law enforcement, a darker chapter in his career has come to light, casting a shadow over his otherwise illustrious reputation. The unresolved case that tragically culminated in suicide has raised questions about Detective Winston's investigative prowess and the toll that unsolved mysteries can take on both victims and those tasked with seeking justice.

At the centre of the controversy is an unsolved case that Detective Winston was assigned to investigate. Despite his reputation for success, this particular case proved to be an insurmountable challenge. The victim's family, the community, and the public at large were left grappling with the pain of not knowing, while Detective Winston's failure to bring closure became a stain on his otherwise commendable record.

Maura Jones was put in a mental asylum after the conviction of killing her husband Luke Jones, the much-loved Mayor of New York.

Her life was ended in the week of 15 September right after Detective Winston closed his investigation into the Guilty Widow case.

The tragedy of the unsolved case goes beyond the failure to apprehend a perpetrator; it extends to the profound impact on the victim's family. The lack of resolution left them in a perpetual state of grief and uncertainty, unable to find solace or closure. Detective Winston's inability to crack the case has not only failed the victim but has also perpetuated the suffering of those left behind.

Chapter 14
144,000

Casper, Wyoming

"Please state your name for the record," Maxine stated as I listened through the one-way glass in investigation room 2. She was sitting across from a man with a dark long beard, with clothes stained with dark red—whether blood or paint—we didn't know yet.

"Joseph Winter," the broody man answered, voice monotone.

I took a deep breath and watched carefully.

I let Maxine go in to talk to the man and put him off. He had a thing for young women, as seen in all the women he presumably murdered. I wondered if he hit them with a shovel or used another tool from his shed. The ME said he could not distinguish—their whole heads were smashed to a mushy texture, and even I gagged and almost puked when we visited Doctor Ashbery.

Truth is Maxine surpassed my interrogation skills—by now I was old enough to have some grey hair showing through my stubble and hair. It was almost time for me to retire and enjoy my last years of solitude.

But not yet—we had one more killer to catch.

"Are you confessing to murdering Cara and Mia Jenkins?" Maxine added.

I leaned on the railing near the window and stared at the man through the glass. He was looking at Maxine with a little glint in his eyes. That evil glint was telling me she would potentially be one of his victims. Maybe he would grab her off the street or on her morning run, or even if she was in a small bar. He would put his sleazy hands on her and she would scream—but it was New York, and no one cared.

I wish I could come over there and punch him for that. This psycho was maybe the worst we've ever encountered.

Joseph Winter was a dear follower of Jehovah's Witnesses here in Wyoming. We expected him to be quiet and order us to call his lawyer, but turns out he didn't have anyone waiting on standby. We picked him up from his house earlier this afternoon and brought him straight into this investigation room. We let him sweat a little before the local detective finally agreed to let Maxine take charge of the questioning. It took us precisely two arguments and one beer to settle.

"I am innocent. I only did what was asked of me," the man responded. He had a monotone voice. No fear or stress. He looked like he was bored out of his mind.

"Christ, another nut-job," the local detective said next to me.

He rolled his eyes and exited the room.

I hated detectives like this; the ones who decluttered through people like they were furniture—the ones who didn't listen. And I know that best because I was one of them. Before Maxine and Chief Kalman—who's enjoying his margarita in Ibiza with his wife, Max's mom—I was exactly like that.

But at some point, in our lives, we must look back and leave *whoever* we were in the past, and become a better version of ourselves.

"Your fingerprints were found on the scene of the crime. Are you telling me you didn't kill those girls, and almost a dozen more?" Maxine shouted. I could feel a slight ring in my ears.

"I did everything I was told—I am a reflection of my god," he almost recited, but there was a small hint in his voice—he sounded excited.

Maxine looked at me through the glass, and as if she could read my mind, she stood up and left the investigation room.

I could hear her angry footsteps in the hallway, and then the door to my side of the glass opened and almost created a dent in the wall from the strong impact.

"This is the third time I'm asking him if he did it and look at this bastard," Maxine gritted through her teeth. She had a vendetta against these psychos and I couldn't blame her.

"He will break."

"No, he won't and we both know it. This is a game for him. Do you think he cares if he ends up in jail? Fuck no."

"Go back and ask him about his religion. He will break," I repeated. We knew Joseph was a Jehovah's Witness and I couldn't help but imagine a small cult of criminals forming inside of a very religious part of the city.

"Oh, god." She rolled her eyes and left the room. I heard the door opening again, and now I closed my eyes.

The motive wouldn't be in his expression, but it'd be in his voice.

That's all that was left—body movement, but he was restrained to the point where he couldn't move.

"Are you a Jehovah's Witness?" Maxine questioned.

"Yes. Born and raised," his voice was higher now, signalling he was proud and confident in his answer.

I opened my eyes and saw Maxine staring right at me. Even though she couldn't see me, I nodded my head and she got back to questioning. Sometimes, people need a slight push or a small nod for full confidence.

"You say you committed all of these listed crimes as an act of God, does God talk to you often?"

"God sends my assignments to me—I haven't had the honour to talk to him myself. We believe he will come one day." Maxine's shoulders sagged. We couldn't prove he was mentally ill. He had acted out on his intentions—no voices, no shadowy figures, and no imaginary leader talking to him. Sometimes, we hoped even the most twisted people were just mentally ill and not psychopaths and sociopaths.

"Are you confessing to the murders of the people I listed before?" Maxine asked for the fifth time.

"I am a humble servant of my god—what he tells me to do, I do—without question." Maxine cocked her head. "I won't confess to anything. I am simply a servant." He smiled—he had one of those sinister smiles where you couldn't tell if he was being sarcastic or not.

"This is the time to state your plea. We have you here as a suspect if you don't understand the weight of this situation." Maxine chuckled. "I put men like you behind bars every day—my question is why did you do it?" She impatiently bounced her leg.

"You won't ever get it, Max," I whispered to myself. The door next to me flew open again, but this time it was our new chief.

Chief Barnes was as far from Kalman as he could be.

He was young and ambitious. He loved golf and black coffee—and he seemed to love looking over my shoulder the most.

"How is the investigation coming together?" He observed the situation.

"He's still intact. Maxine didn't sink her claws in him yet," I offered him a tight-lipped smile and came closer to the glass, trying to shake off the stare Barnes gave me.

Oh, and one more thing—we went to the academy together.

Let's say, I was far more favourite around girls than he was even his own wife. Oops.

"I have pressure on my back from the government. They want this solved as soon as possible."

It wasn't usual that the chief went with us on these trips. It was always me and Max, but now, seemingly we were like new-borns. He just couldn't leave us alone.

"Winston, I want Maxine out of there. I need a confession out of him. I don't need this girl crap." He scoffed and I'm sure he even rolled his eyes.

I turned around, back facing the window. "This isn't girl crap, chief." I came closer to him to assert my power—because I had way more than him.

"Maxine and I do this every time. We crack them open like an egg, and from the intel we collect and we build a profile. We ask the why's and when's and who's. Not your governmental suits. We catch the bad guys, not the politicians sitting on their chairs and fucking their secretaries. So, why don't you go back to your office and look at blank papers and drink your coffee? I'm sure you're way more needed there." I patted him on the back and again turned in Maxine's direction.

"We will get you the proof you need to put him behind bars. But we will understand this excuse of a man first," I said as he was leaving the room.

"The ice you're standing on is really thin. Make sure you find some shelter before hell breaks loose. And I promise you, it will," he muttered the last part over his shoulder and left the room.

I rolled my eyes at his words but they were wandering in my mind. No time for overthinking.

"This is your last chance to plead guilty. Maybe we can get you a reduced sentence. You know, they give those away if you're mentally ill—oh, not ill, disturbed. Sorry, it mixes in here." Maxine laughed as she pointed to her forehead. Sometimes, the best way to approach a psychopath is to become one.

"I am my God's humble servant," he repeated like a chant.

"Yeah, whatever he tells you, you do. I get it—we all get it." Maxine abruptly stood up, raising her eyebrows slightly and exiting the room. I could feel she was becoming tired of him repeating the same phrase all over again, just like I was. Maybe this wouldn't be as easy as we thought.

"Okay, imagine I'm crazy," I said to Maxine as we lay on my couch, sipping the stale beer from my fridge.

"Not that hard." She giggled as she sipped on her fruity wine.

She wasn't the type to drink beer or smoke—only in emergency cases. I guess this one hasn't escalated that high yet.

I had a slight hitch to my voice. "What is the reason why a profound Catholic man would start killing most of his neighbours?"

"He kept mentioning God, but he never clarified which one." Maxine took a swig out of her wine bottle.

"What do you mean by that?" I asked.

"Well, Winston, you wouldn't believe it, but there are more religions than Christianity. Some follow God, some follow a random man who claims to be God," she teased and I tensed my shoulders.

"Maxine." I shook my head at her to start being serious again.

"Maybe he's just following orders. There are many religions that branch from Jehovah's Witnesses. Maybe he's a part of some group."

"I thought groups wanted to be famous."

"Not if you want to still end up on the list." Maxine shrugged.

"What list?" I cinched my eyebrows together. The wrinkle between them started to appear as prominent.

"If you're a part of Jehovah's Witnesses, you believe that you're going to be the one in 144,000 people who are to be saved from doom. That's their motto—just like Christians have their hell and heaven, Jehovah's have this." Maxine draped a small blanket on her lap.

"Were all of them Jehovah's?" I opened the first murder file and Maxine started to open and check the other ones.

"Yes, seems like they even went to the same church." She crossed her arms and leaned back into the couch.

"You think this has to do something with religion?" I asked.

Maxine shook her head.

"If it did, why wouldn't he start earlier? I mean he's old now for starting to kill. If it was religion, I think it would've shown sooner." Maxine scratched the side of her nose—she always does this when she's deep in thought.

I agreed. Either we were wrong about the profile of our killer or his motive, and Winter in that investigation room wasn't going to give us anything other than the words he kept reciting repeatedly.

He's clever, I'll give him that.

"What about the words he keeps reciting? Do we have any clue if they're made up or if they are connected to some religious branch of Jehovah's Witnesses?" By us, I meant myself, Maxine, and her handy friend, Bran.

We worked with Bran on some other cases before. He was handy because he kept quiet most of the time and had no problem digging as deep as the dark web went. We would call Bran and he would laugh and say this was 'fun' for him.

I never really talked to the guy, but he seemed like he wouldn't be the betraying kind.

On one side, I was worried. He wasn't a part of the police force—Bran was a freelancer.

We paid him a heavy sum every time to keep quiet—but I couldn't stop overthinking whether he already knew who I was. I guess after all it's not so hard to find out. On the other side, I didn't really care. If he hadn't told Maxine and the whole world yet, I was safe—like with Kalman.

"Should I call him? I think he's not working today." Maxine reached for her phone but looked at me before dialling Bran's number. She knew how I felt about technology. I barely even had a phone these days. If you wanted to reach me, you knew where I lived—and if you didn't know where I lived, you weren't supposed to contact me.

Maxine stood up when I first heard Bran's voice come from the other side of the phone. She walked to the kitchen and turned her back on me.

She was still secretive with me—unknowingly to the fact I knew her like the back of my hand. I guess I had to, considering I needed to keep my secret a secret. I didn't need her finding out.

"He will be here in less than an hour." Maxine laid her phone on the table carefully, and she took a handful of the stale chips I had on my table. Her face scrunched in disgust when she started to chew them.

Bran arrived earlier than we expected. He was at the apartment in less than ten minutes and didn't even knock.

I heard my front door opening and I laid a hand on my gun on the table, waiting for shots coming from my hallway. Bran stuck his head in—he didn't even bother to take his shoes off.

"Don't shoot me, you psycho." Bran was strictly a pacifist. Even the sight of a gun made him nauseous. I tucked my gun back into the back of my belt and sat back. He opened his computer and looked at the whiteboard filled with colourful scribbles.

"Thanks for coming," I muttered as Maxine appeared in the door frame.

"I thought you said it would take you an hour?" She ruffled his hair and went to sit next to me.

We quickly explained the situation to Bran.

"We have this guy in custody. He's a part of Jehovah's Witnesses. He keeps reciting the words, "I am a humble servant of my god—what he tells me to do, I do." We thought you could dig around the net and find if there is any group that resonated with this slogan." Maxine pushed the glass of water that used to be hers toward Bran.

"I'll do my best. I'll need a few minutes, so please, don't mind me." He started to type on his small computer rapidly. The first time he arrived he hacked into my Wi-Fi and my camera systems in my apartment.

No one could do that, until him.

While Maxine left for the other room, I scooted closer to Bran.

"Do you know?" I cocked my eyebrow.

"I know *everything*, remember that." His expression went from smiley to cold in a matter of seconds. Was he also my enemy?

"I'll keep my mouth shut because of Maxine, but Winston, your time is *running out*. There are people who want you to pay—and not only with your job," he warned quietly.

I nodded and scooted back into my designated spot on the couch. He was right—they were all right—my time was running out.

It took Bran almost an hour before he lifted his head from his computer. I looked at him, and he nodded at me.

"Maxine." I shook her shoulder. She fell asleep on my couch again. "We have a lead." She mumbled incoherently and straightened up. She had a small sleep mark on her cheek.

Bran spoke up when she appeared in the doorframe. "There seems to be a group online—a chat, if you will. Your guy seems to be a part of it, along with 36 other members who are scattered all over the world. But they have been talking about meeting. Seems like you have a week to find enough evidence and gear up because they're coming right into this town. And there seems to be a little party."

"A party? Why would they…" Maxine didn't finish her sentence.

"A sacrifice," Bran clarified, and I could see his throat bob dryly.

"Christ," Maxine added.

"We need to break this guy. Any dirt on him?" I closed my eyes, waiting for the worst.

"His daughter went missing a little under a year ago."

"When the murders started," Me and Maxine said in unison.

This man must've been the leader of this group, otherwise, why would he be the main killer?

"Imagine how many more bodies are all over America." Maxine almost read my thoughts. I took a deep breath in and out to try and calm myself.

We dealt with the usual psychos, but never a group as big as this. Bran later revealed that these weren't only men—they were active families and spouses of important people.

"Thank you, Bran; I don't think you know how much you helped," I heard Maxine say as she went to let Bran out of my apartment. He nodded his head but said nothing. Maxine hugged him and opened the door, which she locked after he left.

"So, Bran," I teased Maxine. He was way too old for her but still.

"I'm really looking forward to contacting one of your ex-wives and asking about your sex life." She puckered her lips and blew me a kiss. I rolled my eyes and laughed.

Five days after Bran gave us all the evidence we needed, we still weren't any closer to getting any information out of our suspect. We offered him water and food but he always declined. He was trained for these interviews, which took us way too long to figure out in the first place.

"We're not breaking him," Maxine deducted.

I nodded and sighed.

"You have that look on your face again," she mumbled.

"What face?"

"The 'I'm going to do something stupid and get myself killed' face." She gave me a worried look.

"That only happened twice," I defended myself.

"Twice is too much already." I walked around the room and looked out of the window. I could see the small streets with houses and thought about all the innocent people who were murdered in the process of this group. They even called themselves the Sons of Salvation.

I spoke up. "We need to let him go."

"Excuse me?" Max's mouth formed an O shape.

"Look at him. He's prepared for every question, he has an alibi, and he hasn't had a drink of water in days. He expected all of this. We have to surprise him." I turned around to face Maxine.

She walked around the room for a couple of minutes—running scenarios in her head—and then nodded.

"If this man kills another person, it's on you." She pointed a finger in my chest and shook her head with disappointment. I felt the same way, but my gut told me this was the only way.

I took the role of telling Joseph he was being released. The expression on his face told me I was right—he was surprised, although he masked it well. His eyes widened and his brows knitted together for a fraction of a second until he put his expressionless face on again.

"I'm free to go? No charges?"

"Yes, Mr Winter, we apologise for the inconvenience. We already found the suspect and have him in custody." I smiled at him.

"Thank you, Detective," he muttered before a fellow officer escorted him out of the building.

Four men were already following him, and we had Bran tap his phone so we could see what was happening. We could see when he woke up, where he went, who he was with—and mostly, what he said in that chat room.

After 24 hours had passed, Joseph Winter thought he was safe again and decided to message the group that he would, in fact, take part in the sacrifice. We were already sitting in our gear in my car when Maxine decided to speak up.

"I've been keeping something from you for a long time," she admitted.

"Me too, but now isn't the time." I put my gloved hand on her for a few seconds to show her I was genuine and signalled my radio.

"How are we looking, boys?" I muttered on my radio. The other receiver replied in a second, telling me we were still waiting for the signal.

We sat in silence for the next two minutes, until I saw the small light coming from the other car in Morse Code intervals. We needed to move in.

I opened my car door silently and started to move closer to the house. Maxine was behind me, with more detectives.

I followed Team 1 who were a little faster than us. We signalled to each other with our hands, making sure to be as quiet as possible. We were moving closer to an abandoned barn, which had some orange light glowing from inside of it. We could hear some chanting from the inside.

Everything happened *so* fast after.

We infiltrated the barn and saw people dancing naked with children present. I shivered at the sight. We beset them from every side, every entrance covered, and when one of the men dancing saw us, he screamed so loud my ears hurt. Some people didn't stop dancing and moving in a circle, so the other team fired one warning shot to the ceiling of the barn.

People stopped moving but they were still muttering little chants under their breaths. They turned to face us, the fire inside the circle still burning bright. From the corner of my eye, I could see Maxine's hand on the trigger—ready to end this.

In less than a second, and before I could blink, all of the people in the circle started to run at us. Naked and armless they screamed and before I could open my mouth to scream 'Don't shoot' they were all lying on the ground. Children were screaming, men were confused and Maxine gagged at the sight of the blood draining from the lifeless bodies.

"This was planned. They played us," I muttered as I lowered my weapon and whipped my head to check at Maxine who was leaving the barn already. The tactical team was also leaving, making space for the detectives arriving with the medics—sadly, there was no one left to be saved.

"You good?" I asked Maxine who doubled down and fell to her knees. She was heaving up her puke and coughing at the same time. I knelt next to her and rubbed her back—even after years of seeing blood, she still got nauseous.

And to be completely honest, I didn't blame her. The sight inside that barn would make a skilled psychopath puke.

"This was suicide. Planned suicide. How come we didn't know?" She mumbled as she brushed her bangs away from her sweaty forehead.

"I know. We tried," I mumbled and she shook her head.

"We should've tried harder." She sniffled.

A few hours later, we were back in New York. We flew back with the other agents that came with us from New York, including the new chief.

Bran even showed up and requested to be with us. I sat together with Maxine, and Bran sat opposite me.

"I found more chats. Some I didn't find before because they weren't active or used in years, but you were right. They planned this group suicide and even left a note." He looked over at Maxine who was sleeping peacefully.

Chief Barnes was staring at the back of my head the entire flight. I tried to shake off his stare but couldn't. Bran slid a small silver flash drive over to my side of the table.

"It's time to leave, Winston—or perhaps finally face your crimes. He's close," Bran whispered and looked over at the seat Chief Barnes sat in.

"Thank you." I had no idea what was on the flash drive, but I hoped it was the digital evidence of my crime.

And he was right—my time officially ran out.

Chapter 15
The Trial

The Trial
New York

I was 18 when I first killed a man.

My whole life, I've been lying to everyone—including myself. I thought, maybe, no one would find out. But the truth is I was as bad as the men I've been chasing after all these years. No matter how many of them I would put behind bars, one day, one of them would be my cellmate. And no matter how many times I thought to myself, *It's time.* It was truly never the time—until now.

After my last conversation with Bran, I knew my time had run out. No more lying to Maxine or Barnes. I knew if I told someone, they would one day turn on me and start talking, which is why in all these years, only one person knew—and that was Chief Kalman.

Chief Kalman helped me to hide my secret because he knew why I did it. He knew what my foster parents did to me. And he vowed to keep my secret and never tell anyone. And he kept his word.

But getting rid of two bodies wasn't exactly easy—but it wasn't harder than lying to everyone my whole life. Maxine, all my wives, and every family we have helped will be sitting behind their TVs when they hear that the infamous Detective Winston is in fact a *stone-cold killer.*

But as Bran said, my time was running out.

Many people will wonder; why didn't I run? I've been running for most of my life, and I was tired of it. I just hoped I wouldn't see Maxine in that courtroom next week.

On Monday morning, I got a knock on my door. I was in the middle of packing all my belongings in two boxes when Chief Kalman showed up. Before speaking up, he scanned my apartment. I didn't let him know it was time for me to give myself to the authorities.

He whipped around and looked at me with a worried expression. "You can leave. We have enough money to…"

"I'm tired of running, Mark. I ran so far and look, that night never erased itself from my mind." I pointed my finger to the side of my head and he shook his head. "Every corner I turn, I hope I won't see his or her face again. They ruined me," I pleaded. "No matter how far I moved away or how many times I tried to forget—they won't ever leave me. I took their life and now I have to carry it inside of me forever."

"It doesn't have to end like this. You're a good cop." He sat down on my worn-out couch and held his head in his hands. "We can find a way…" He stopped talking when he saw my relaxed expression.

"I'm okay with this. I'm not being forced. It's time." I tried to soothe him by rubbing his shoulder. He was still tense.

Kalman was like a father to me—he taught me how to tie my own tie, showed me how to shave, and introduced me to the academy—he gave me a chance at life. And we had a good run.

It's been almost 35 years since that night.

The faded cigarette burns on my arms were covered by heaps of random tattoos. I told the artist to just cover them as much as possible and he did. Even from a close distance, you couldn't tell they were underneath the layers of ink.

That night was engraved in my mind and on my body, no matter how hard I tried to hide it. It haunted me while I slept—sometimes when I looked in the mirror, I would still see the splatters of blood.

"You're a good man, Winston. No matter what happened that night, you will always be remembered as a good man. Whatever the judge says, everyone will know," he comforted me.

"No, Mark. I'm the worst of them all. No matter who comes to testify, I still committed the crime. I'll go away for a long time and no matter what you or Maxine will say at the stand will make people believe that I had a good reason to do it—hell, is there even a good reason to commit manslaughter?" I shook my head and I could feel my heart beat out of my chest.

"You…" Mark took a deep breath. "You solved *so many* crimes, Winston. You put bad men behind bars and you did it because you wanted to help the world. Not because you were bored or searching for that feel of rush and thrill. You did it so people around you would be safe."

I didn't let him finish his monologue.

"I am a bad man, Mark. No matter how many people will be waiting to kill me in jail, I still committed the crime." I handed him a small box with framed pictures and a couple of filled diaries from my past.

"Make sure no one makes a garage sale with these, okay?" I swear I had tears in my eyes as I handed him the small box. He looked inside and flipped the picture frames to see what was set inside.

Gather yourself, Winston. My brain reminded me.

"Call Maxine and tell her to go into the archive and find file #34657. It has my parents on that file and tell her she will need Bran for this. Please don't tell her anything else—I don't want her to know. I also don't want her on the case. Make sure it's taken care of." I pursed my lips together in a tight line, showing Mark I was serious. I knew they were family, but this was more important than keeping up relations with your stepdaughter.

God, I just wished she wouldn't be mad.

On the morning of 24 May, I was arrested in my apartment.

There were no news vans out front, which I was immensely thankful for. Barnes showed up, as well as Kalman, but I couldn't see Maxine anywhere—seems like Kalman listened to me.

It must've felt…weird, putting your own colleague in the back of the police car. I was handcuffed for the first time in my life. They recited the same passage I used to recite; you have the right to remain silent. If you do say anything, what you say can be used against you in a court of law. You have the right to consult with a lawyer and have that lawyer present during any questioning. If you cannot afford a lawyer, one will be appointed for you if you so desire.

It felt refreshing, to see the backs of my colleague's heads. I never truly understood what was so scary about sitting in the back—but now I understood.

It was the eerie feeling that you were about to be locked up, maybe forever.

The car ride was silent. I understood. I wasn't their colleague or the icon I used to be. I remind myself of what Kalman told me when he found me all those years ago.

"You killed a man. You killed a woman. No matter how many good dreams you will have, one bad will come your way and you will be a wreck. You can hide and change your name, move away, or try and have a family—but you won't ever forget the feeling of your knife cutting through all the layers of skin. That feeling, it won't go away."

And he was right.

They took me in and I went through the usual process. They took my picture, put my gun into evidence, and took my fingerprints. I could see the whole department lurking behind the frosted windows. No sight of the blonde and no sight of Barnes either. I was still cuffed, being dragged into an interrogation room by two unknown cops. They must've been new.

"Sit down," one cop ordered me, and I obliged. I wasn't one to follow rules, but I didn't want to make this more difficult than it had to be.

Imagine how embarrassing it would be if I made a mess inside.

"So, who's on my case?" I tried to make myself comfortable on the wooden chair, but it was designed to make people inside it uncomfortable. I was always used to being on the other side of the glass, and when I see my expression in the mirror I can't decipher if I'm truly ready to face my crimes.

"Shut up," the cop who was cuffing me spoke up for the first time. I wonder what they must've been thinking.

I kept quiet.

They left me sitting there for about 20 minutes in complete silence until I heard the first small sound. A rhythmic tap of heeled boots on the floor raised an alarm in my head. The only person who wears heeled boots in this precinct. The doors opened with the most force.

"You son of a bitch." Maxine stood at her full height and kept shaking her head at me, cuffs on my hands and my fingertips still blackened from the ink they rubbed on them to take my fingerprints.

She didn't even sit down. She threw the file on the table and banged the glass twice, signalling for anyone sitting inside to scramble. She waited, unmoving until the door from the other side closed. She leaned over the table and slapped me hard.

She slapped me so hard I could taste blood in my mouth. I swallowed.

"You know, I always deep down knew you weren't just an average man with an average life." She laughed. Her laugh was genuine, but it didn't last as long as I imagined. "You played me." She scoffed.

"I did no such thing…"

"A fucking decade. You *lied* straight to my face every day for almost a decade. And you know what's the worst thing about it?"

I kept quiet. I had nothing to say that would justify my actions.

"I had no idea. I could look through psychopaths and sociopaths and murderers but not you." I could see her eyes glistening under the yellow light. She wore an uncoordinated outfit, which told me someone pulled her out of bed not long ago.

Despite my excellent plan on how to get myself in jail, I couldn't tell Maxine why I did what I did. I didn't want her to be another bystander who was going to recite their 'I'm sorry; it must've been so hard' speech which will change nothing and help no one.

"I want another detective," I tried to talk with a neutral voice, but mine betrayed me and broke at the end of my sentence.

"Sad. You will have to deal with me. And I'm going to shoot you if you don't explain it to me. Start now." She grabbed her gun out of her belt holster and put it on the table with a warning glance.

My silence angered her further. She grabbed the gun and cocked it and pointed it in my direction.

"Start singing or you will be wheeled out of here and put straight into a black ambulance. I will personally make sure of that." I knew Maxine's anger, but this wasn't just anger. This was her revenge for me.

I kept my head low for a few minutes, sitting in utter silence.

"You know that I'm an orphan. What you don't know is that my parents didn't die when I turned 18. I lied. I never actually knew them."

Maxine hesitated but she put her gun down. She had this skill—she could tell when people were lying. I was genuine.

My composure was hanging by a thread. My heart kept beating against my rib-cage—kept telling me to tell her the truth; she would understand.

But truthfully, I couldn't take that chance.

"I was put through hell, Maxine. I just want you to know that if I saw another choice…"

"You mean to tell me you wouldn't kill two people if there was 'a way'?" She looked at me with a desperate expression. Understanding me must've been hard, considering her position as a cop and my friend.

But, were we friends? After all, I was now what she despised most. No friendship can survive this, not even ours. And what's worse, she looked at me as if she knew; deep down, that I wasn't that bad.

"Winston." She snapped her fingers in front of my face. I must've disassociated again.

"Kalman talked to me. He…He explained to me. He explained why you did it—I just need to hear you say it. This might be the last time I see you." She cleared her throat, and her question hurt more than any of the burns or slashes on my body.

"Are you a bad guy?" Her fingertips grabbed my cold hand.

I squinted my eyes. I looked away from her and took a deep breath.

Was I a bad guy?

Define bad guy. Bad guy is a man who hurts children and women. Bad guy snitches when he sees someone less fortunate steal food from a supermarket. Bad guy golfs while people die. Bad guy doesn't care about animals or climate change.

And although I was none of those things, I still belonged to that category.

"If it was self-defence like Kalman said, why did you hide it?" Maxine let go of my hand a while ago, but I could now feel the cold edge of her voice.

"It wasn't self-defence—I mean it was, but not officially. I was abused for years and I just couldn't handle it anymore. I couldn't handle the feeling of my sore throat after screaming while my father used his belt to whip me like a pig. I still feel the pain—I can still feel the burning of my own fucking flesh, Maxine. It's tattooed in my brain. Every single time you asked me why I wore a long sleeve shirt when you were sweating in a tank top; look underneath my shirt and you will see." I motioned for her to grab my hands and see. I laid them in front of her, palms flat on the table.

I could see the battle in her mind—to believe, or to not believe?

For a second, I thought she would close the file and leave the room, and leave me here to rot forever. I couldn't bear to look at the expression on her face, so I looked away.

She didn't walk away. She didn't move an inch until she raised the sleeve of my shirt. There were some scars the tattoo artist couldn't cover, no matter how hard he tried. Those same scars that haunted me every night were now going to be engraved in Maxine's mind.

"You still lied," she admitted while letting go of the sleeve—slowly—as if I was now made of sugar and could fall apart at the slightest touch.

"Because of this." My hands were restrained so I couldn't motion between us.

"See how you touched me? How do you now see that I am a victim of a crime? You'll start treating me like a child—but I am not helpless, Maxine. I killed those two, and if you want to know, I'd do it again in a heartbeat." I snarled at her.

She shook her head, but I saw it in her eyes—just like she saw that I've been telling her the truth.

"You liked me as the fearless detective, the iconic man who brought down crime organisations and killed the bad guy every time—how would you feel knowing I was the next bad guy you were going to hunt?" I breathed out.

"I trusted you!" She screamed at me.

"You can still trust me, kid. I didn't change in the last 24 hours." She rubbed her eyes.

"You did."

"I'm the same Winston you used to be best friends with. I still have a cheap beer in my fridge and the bad smoking habit you hated. Nothing changed. The killer has always been there. I was *always* the bad guy; it just took you years to see."

"You are the worst of them all, Winston—you know why? Because I knew you. I would vouch for you, hell, I'd even put my own life on the line for you—and you turned out like this. My partner would never do this." And with the angry tone stopped, I opened my eyes and she was gone.

Gone forever.

In the next hour, I was offered two deals.

A tall, lanky man appeared in front of me with a thick file and a big briefcase.

He was the epitome of a Wall Street lawyer—he had the gelled hair and the coffee addiction—without even looking at him, I knew he was cheating on his wife with at least three women.

"Well, well," he tsked with his tongue and raised his eyebrows, showing off his prominently wrinkled forehead. "I'll give you a little rundown of what can happen next." And oh boy, he did.

One, I would have to work very hard with this celebrity-looking lawyer and present a case of abuse from my two deceased 'parents'. I'd play the ugly duckling and sell a lie about what truly happened that night. He said my chances of being on probation were high after acting out this telenovela.

I, obviously, declined.

"Are you suicidal by any chance?" Robert, my lawyer, asked. He was sipping on his second coffee, and the more I looked at him, the more I could see the faint outline of the purple half-moons under his eyes. Either he's the best lawyer or he's having some trouble keeping up with the company and clients.

"No."

"Then why in god's name are you trying to get yourself into jail?" He raised his eyebrows again. Maybe he should invest in Botox instead of gifts for his mistress.

"Look, Robert. I'm done. I don't want probation or a short minimum-security stay in a small prison. I can't work my old job and my family hates me now." I didn't even have a family in the first place. "So, no. I won't act like I'm innocent. Give me option two." I cleared my throat.

Option two consisted of someone finding evidence of my crime. Now, all they had was my confession and a cold file box. When Bran handed me that USB drive, I plugged it into my computer, and with the help of a YouTube manual, I was looking at the pictures of a crime scene. The only thing that made this crime scene different from any other one was that it was set in my small child-like bedroom.

A blue rug with small white dots. A small bed—at some point in my stay, I couldn't fit in it anymore—but that wasn't ever an issue.

Although I despised the room, the whole house, and them, I still looked at the pictures of my childhood room with a small glint of adoration. How I still managed to make it so cosy and homey while I was beaten every single day into a pulp, wiping my blood and tears into the small comforter.

I got adopted when I was seven. The whole neighbourhood came to watch me get out of the car. For a seven-year-old, I was small.

We weren't fed like the other kids were.

I loved this room. I spent hours inside and even now after all these years, I was still staring at it. When I clicked so the next picture would show, I was met with the bloodbath I caused. I sliced my father's hands off, to make sure he wouldn't try to hurt me with them again. I stabbed him with a small kitchen knife that I kept underneath my pillow—each time he would come into my room I told myself I would use it on him and stop him from hurting me further, but it took me years to gather up the courage to do it.

And that night, I was done.

"I'll take the second option," I said without hesitating.

"No. You will get 24 hours to choose. I don't want you to regret it—no matter what you say now, guilt and fear will seep into your thoughts and it will make you choose option one. Believe me, detective; I see fearless men like you fall to their knees and cry when they hear their sentence length. And what's worse, is seeing all those people sitting on those uncomfortable chairs for hours waiting for your sentence to be served—you don't ever want to hear what it does to families. They cry and scream and kick, wishing they could've stopped you. Or perhaps no one will show up for you." He grabbed his belongings and left.

"I wish," I silently whispered and lay on the cold table.

Once you enter the investigation zone, you shouldn't have any visitors.

"Winston, wake the fuck up," I heard Maxine's voice as she shook me. I thought I was dreaming. It hasn't even been six hours since she left—and she brought an army.

My loyal friend Doctor Ashbery stood in one corner of the room; Maxine stood next to Kalman in the middle. And in the other corner stood my third ex-wife, who charged at me and slapped me with all the force she had.

"You women love slapping, don't you?" I sucked in the side of my cheek and Ashbery let out a small laugh but quickly fell silent when Maxine and my ex-wife showed him the middle finger.

"You shouldn't be here." I lay on the table again, waiting for them to leave this room.

"Oh, fuck you," Carrie snarled.

"Shut up," Maxine agreed.

Kalman and Ashbery just looked at me with a worried expression. I seriously doubt how Kalman kept my secret intact when less than a day after I made him promise to leave everyone out of it, he went out and ran his mouth to every available ear.

"We are all here to help." Ashbery laid a hand on Maxine's shoulder to calm her down, while Carrie stared at me with venom in her eyes.

"I married a fucking psycho," Carrie mumbled.

Maxine's head whipped back. "Tell me about that." She shook her head and returned her attention to me.

"This is how it's going to go." Maxine brushed her hair that covered her forehand back and clipped it with a small clip that had a bow on it. I immediately recognised it as a gag gift I got her a couple of months ago, a week after she got bangs.

"You will not rot in jail. We will get you out. We will prove it was self-defence." She held her finger up when I tried to speak. "Shut up and listen. Now, we need you to exactly tell us what happened that night. Leave no detail behind. I want to know what the temperature was, what the clock said and how the air felt when you breathed in. I want to go back there, Winston. And none of us care if you protest. If you want to protest, we brought Carrie to rip your head from your neck. Deal?" Maxine smiled.

Carrie, from the corner of the room, mumbled 'fuck you' to me once again. Kalman and Ashbery whipped out their notebooks and started to write things as I started to speak.

"The month was November. The air was cold as hell. Rural Nebraska, 35 years ago was even sadder than it is now." I gulped. Maxine's hand came to warm up my own.

No matter what was going to happen, I knew my family wouldn't stop until they proved me innocent of my crime.

Chapter 16
Sanning

Sanning
New York

I was 16 when I first killed a man.

Yes, I lied again—it happens.

Humans are far from perfect, but my two-year criminal career was pretty damn close if you ask me. I got by without raising an alarm, always wore gloves to prevent my fingerprints from showing up, and even shaved my hair to mask my appearance.

My plan was *perfect*.

I planned everything until the last detail—meeting an officer who had an interest in young troubled cadets whom he thought he could fix, meeting the therapist Carrie, who wanted nothing more but to dig deep into my brain and find out what happened that day—and how could I forget dear Maxine, the genius who never found out. I gave her so many clues, but she never caught on. I guess she's not as good as everyone says she is.

These idiots were willing to help me get out of jail, for Christ's sake. Unknowingly, they thought I was innocent—in my opinion, I did nothing but rid this world of even more criminals.

If I had to keep count, I put around 130 guilty men and women into jail. If you count my seven victims with that, it's almost 140. That must count for something.

You might ask how one starts their criminal career so young.

And the truth is, I didn't.

The criminal career found me.

One thing I didn't lie about was getting almost beaten to death by my stepfather. I could still point out the bruises which were now healed. I remembered exactly where they were—for years, I traced my small nimble fingers around the big blue and purple-coloured skin. I remember there wasn't an inch he didn't touch.

But one day, I was old enough to realise this wasn't my fault. It was not my fault every time someone angered him; I got to be the little toy he could beat to a pulp. I don't believe that it was my fault his slashes across my back still tingled when I saw a puddle of blood or someone's head getting chopped off.

So, one day, I don't remember the exact date, I went out. I was attending the local school, where everyone turned a blind eye to all the fresh bruises on my hands and face, I carried after each weekend or holiday break.

I found a group of kids who were considered a bad influence and I joined their small clique. It didn't take them long to figure out that I was meaner than I appeared and I fit inside their small circle perfectly. One thing led to another, one handshake led to another and I met Charlie.

Charlie's father was a local cop, corrupted beyond the word and who brought home files from cold cases that didn't fit into the archives, which were fuller than ever. For 40 dollars, I got 60 scans of fingerprints from old cases—preferably those of criminals who were still alive and at large, running from the police.

These fingerprints made sure that the police had a suspect—*"if you killed a man, it was only a question of time to when and where you would kill again"*—said Charlie, whose father repeated that to him almost every day. With Charlie's help, I acquired knowledge about how the system worked. I never told him about my plan which would be too risky. I was young, and so was he, and he would probably run straight to his daddy and sing to him.

Acquiring a gun in America leaves too much of a paper trail, so I decided a knife from their kitchen, which I wasn't even allowed to be in, would suffice.

Even though I cannot remember the exact date when I killed my foster parents, I can clearly remember the weather outside. It was a cold night at the start of August. I think it might've been close to my birthday. Remembering that night was easy yet hard. I was conflicted and sometimes I couldn't tell between the reality of what truly occurred and what my mind made up as a defence mechanism.

I used to curl up in a ball and shiver every night in winter. No one offered me tea or a small blanket. I was underweight and too short, which intrigued my 15-year-old classmates to bully me.

I waited patiently until they both fell asleep—and although my foster mother didn't do anything to me, I still held a vendetta against her. Maybe it was the fact that she didn't do anything. She just wailed in her room when she heard my screams and never got the courage to confront my foster father about it.

"Boys don't cry," he used to say. And so, at some point, I stopped crying. I stopped showing any emotion in that household.

The only time I felt good after that was when my foster father woke up tied to a chair. His hands were tied behind his back and his pyjama was still on. And after a couple of seconds, he regained consciousness and realised what was happening.

"Untie me, you ungrateful little bitch!" He screamed. His screams didn't matter—we lived far from the busy street, and I assumed if no one heard my screams, no one would hear his screams either.

"No, can't do, I'm sorry. It's time you get a taste of my misery." I chuckled when he froze. I guess he already knew about my plan.

"I'm still standing, you know? All those bruises didn't make me any weaker. Quite the opposite—they made me angrier. So, every time you feel the slash across your back or the slap across your face, I hope you get angry. Anger is the *best* feeling in the world, isn't it? I'm sure you know," I hummed. Grabbing the knife from the small kitchen cabinet I slowly lit the lighter and grazed the knife with it.

"This is going to hurt, in all honesty. But it's only temporary." I heard him scream for a split second before I drove the knife through his chest. He had no time to recollect himself because in a moment I was stabbing him again. I made sure to study biology a little harder this year to see which organs are vital and which places on the body hurt the most.

"You," he breathed out after a second. I knelt so our eyes were levelled and I could see my foster mom slowly waking up. I made sure to inject her with a precise dose of some drug my friends gave me to help me 'sleep'.

I shared a small sob story with them a couple of weeks ago, which was half true and half made up. That's my life from now on—half-*truth* and half a *lie*.

"Good morning, sunshine." I gave her the nickname she used after my father left for work. She would call me to eat breakfast with her, sometimes washing all the residue blood and other body liquids off me after his turn ended. That was her way of silently saying sorry. It didn't do anything to me.

"Jakey, please untie us." She even called me by my fake name, how fortunate.

"Don't call me that," I silently told her so he wouldn't hear. I still felt compelled to hurt her—but I didn't want him to get the pleasure of watching.

"Please don't," she begged while another wave of tears washed from her eyes and I wanted to laugh.

"It's too late for begging," I mumbled while I brushed some stray hairs away from her face.

I returned my attention to my father. If you knew him, you'd never guess what kind of a monster he was. But I was lucky enough to see that side of him.

I saw him as the perfect neighbour, I saw him as the perfect cop.

But now, I reduced him to a small puddle of blood and constant angry shouts.

"Why would I stop?" I refused to call him by his name.

"You're mad," he muttered and I let out a small huff of breath.

"I am mad?" I laughed. "You made me go mad," I screamed into his face.

"No matter how much I tried to be good, you still came into my room and took all your anger out on me. No matter how happy you seemed when you came back home, no matter how much sex she gave you." I pointed a finger in my mother's direction. "Do you not see? I am you."

Both of them stilled after they heard me. I landed another hard slap on my father's face, which I could see swelling already. There was some blood dripping on his chin mixed with his spit. I was compelled to wipe it off but I needed him to feel what I felt.

"And you." I moved back to my foster mother. "You're even worse than him." I chuckled.

"You watched me, you heard me cry and still you didn't have enough courage to stop him from hurting me. I was innocent before all of this, but now, look at me." I held her face in my hands and gripped her chin so she could truly see me.

"You made a small innocent boy into a monster. And you truly didn't see it—did you? At least you didn't want to see him like this, so you locked yourself away in your room and lay on your bed and listened to me," I hissed.

"You don't understand," she whispered, looking in her husband's direction.

"Oh, does he *beat* you too? Does he *slap* you around? Well, guess what, you're an adult. You chose him, and you brought me here knowing he was going to beat me and turn me against my morals. But it's okay. After this, we will be even." I turned around and slammed my knife into my father's back. He cried out in agony and for the first time in a long time I felt full of emotion.

"See, I lied again." Walking so I could face his front; I slowly slid my sharp knife across the fat on his neck and his blood soon coated my hands. I stuck my hand into his open throat to gather more and rubbed it all the way from my mother's cheeks to her lips.

"Just know we will never be even." I gritted out, and then it was time for her to get her portion of my revenge.

The jury was already sitting down when I could hear the grand doors open. My whole family, or the four idiots I manipulated into believing me, just arrived. They all looked serious and wore ties and heels to look more professional and truthful.

Doctor Ashbery was giving me a thumbs-up when I offered him the best smile I could come up with. Now that four people were going to testify for me, I was 100% sure I would get out of jail time. They were all looking at me as if I was their God.

Maxine looked worried.

Carrie looked annoyed to be here, but I'll give her points for showing up. Even when we were married, her resting expression was closer to a scowl than a smile.

The judge entered the courtroom—a small petite blonde, who was probably the oldest person in the whole room. Her small heels clicked when they slid on the flooring. The press must be a nightmare for her, as I can imagine. It must be even worse for my lawyer, but he is used to it. He showed up looking like Ken from Barbie, for Christ's sake.

She sat down on her chair, which squeaked. I could feel the whole room tense, and I wasn't even facing those people.

I could just imagine it; Kalman comforting Maxine who refused to even hug him before today, but I'm sure they will bond after they find me innocent again. Doctor Ashbery was taking notes—he once told me he was a 'nerd' for notes. What a joke.

Carrie was looking at her watch when I looked behind me when the judge started to talk about all the formalities.

She straightened her hair, which meant she probably had an appointment with another patient right after my trial.

I knew Carrie like the back of my palm—she and Maxine shared a lot more than just their hair colour.

Carrie was *meticulous*. She could read every expression known to man; except she had no idea I had been constantly lying to her all our marriage. I was the only person she couldn't figure out—no matter how hard she tried. Her personality was a lot different than Maxine's. Carrie liked to compromise. She liked to have exactly half of her things at my apartment and half of the things she owned back in her apartment. She was rich—filthy rich even. When we first met, I was living like a cop on a cop's salary, while she wore Dolce to our first date.

"Please sit down," the judge commanded with a shy voice and we all sat down. She made my lawyer read all the important details and she wrote them down. Next was my cross-examination.

I was asked to sit on the witness stand and state my name. I had to even put my hand on the Bible and swear to God, to tell the truth.

But God never stopped me from lying before.

"Mr Winston, do you think you are innocent?" Another lawyer from the opposing side asked me with a silly tone. I could tell he was young and probably new to the law firm. His mentor was sitting with a calm stoic expression.

"I think I am innocent." I tried to look as scared as possible.

"I lived through so much pain and I saw violence as my last resort. I couldn't know better; I was only 16 years old." I silently chuckled.

"Sixteen?" The judge asked. My calm expression remained. I could see her eyebrows knitting together in confusion.

"Eighteen. I am sorry, Your Honour, I made a mistake. I'm under so much stress." I shook my head and looked up to Maxine. Seeing her expression fall made me want to smirk, but I shook off her stare and remained concentrated on the questions the young lawyer gave me.

The trial was fairly quick considering I was being judged for murdering two people. Robert shouted, "Objection!" a couple of times, but I was ready for all the possible questions the young prosecutor asked me. Before I got arrested, I wrote down the most crucial questions the prosecution might ask me on trial and learned the answers by heart.

I couldn't lose my stand and had some questions throw me off. My calm expression remained carved on my face until the end of the trial.

Each time I sat behind the small fence between the judge and the public, I always spent the whole trial wondering what the jury thought. I tried to analyse their expressions—some of them were easy to read, but others, who I presumed were older and more experienced, never showed one expression. These people were responsible for putting people on death row and such. How can you sleep peacefully after putting a man on death row? Does the thought of his innocence or guilt not keep them up at night?

I guess the same question could be asked of me. But killing a man with my bare hands will always be different from sentencing him to rot in jail and then living through the feeling of knowing when his death will come.

Slow death is the worst—I'd know.

"The jury and the court will regroup in 20 minutes," the judge announced and everyone cleared out. I was left sitting on a small uncomfortable bench. I guess that's what most criminals deserve.

I had this small uncontrollable urge to tell everyone the truth. See how their faces are painted with confusion and how angry Maxine is. I bet she would jump over the table and kill me on the spot.

We're not really that different, you and I.

I saw her blonde hair from the corner of my eyes. She was on the phone, presumably talking to her mother. I scoffed. She's like a child.

I could see her slipping her phone into her pocket. She turned around and marched over to me with confident strides. Sitting on the narrow bench opposite of me, she stilled for a second, contemplating what to say.

"Bran called. He told me you knew this would happen." I could see confusion in her expression. "Why don't you tell me the true version now, not that treatment crap?" It was my turn to still now. I had no idea what to tell her.

"The treatment crap is the truth. But I guess at least orange looks good on me," I joked, pointing to the generic uniform I was wearing, which couldn't be more different than my usual leather jacket and jeans.

"What if they don't pardon you?"

"You were never an optimist, Maxine, were you? Let fate and destiny take care of this. You worry too much about your old man," I teased her.

"There are rumours at work. That you were behind most of these cold cases, that you're a freak...and more insults I won't bring up now." She shrugged carelessly, but I could see she cared about me deeply.

"No matter what gets decided on in the courtroom, I want you to believe in me—you, Kalman, Ashbery, and Carrie. That's the solemn reason why I agreed to this joke of a trial—did you see the young man stuttering up there? I tried so hard not to laugh." I let out a small huff of air and shook my head, pretending.

"You know, no matter what happens, I'll be here for you. If you're guilty or innocent, I know you're not a bad guy," Maxine whispered, so the passing people wouldn't hear.

Oh. The feeling of victory was sizzling in my heart. If Maxine believed my little 'helpless boy' act, then so would everyone else. Maybe I should've pursued a career in show business instead of being a cop. But it wouldn't be as fun as this is.

"Thank you." I nodded while biting my lip. Was it this easy?

As we walked back to the courtroom with Maxine closely following the guards, I wondered if she knew something I wasn't aware of.

I obviously hired a guy to leave some breadcrumbs for Bran, so he wouldn't be too suspicious of why my file and life are so clean.

I was basically the Virgin Mary—I was never arrested, there are no porn videos that include my face or name, and I even donate to a women's shelter every month. I was the perfect man—except for the fact I was divorced three times before and I had almost no friends apart from these four idiots.

The only problem is there might be a small corner of the dark web where someone posted all my foster homes and my pictures and all the aliases I went by for years. But the chances of someone as *silly* as Bran finding those files are close to zero.

One day, he will find them. One day. But I will be far gone by then.

We sat down again. My back was close to hurting from these chairs. The judge kept talking and I tuned her out. I tried to think what could make Maxine so quiet in the back. For the last hour, she was whispering details to either Kalman or Ashbery, but now she was quiet. Maybe she was truly worried about my sentence. Maybe she was worried about how calm and collected I looked. My back was straight as if we were back in fourth grade.

"Has the jury decided on the sentence for Detective Winston?" The judge asked. One man, presumably chosen from the group of judges as the speaker got up and said a simple 'yes'. The way his voice lacked any emotion didn't allow me to try and see if I was truly going to jail or if I was going to be free. Not saying I wouldn't know how to escape from jail—jails are one big maze, but once you recognise the hierarchy and befriend some people, escaping is even easier than it seemed in Prison Break. And I'm sure my four friends wouldn't stop to help me and clear my name.

The judge was given a small letter. It is poetic how one piece of paper can change someone's life so drastically. She opened it, and I could feel my heart beating in my chest. In these few seconds of total silence, I noticed small details about the courtroom and the people sitting inside it.

Like how everyone from the jury looked so generic. No one had any special marks or tattoos on them—they all looked like they were hired. If I didn't know the judge from seeing her work on some of my cases, I would think I was being set up.

Or how comfortable I was with going to jail knowing I sent almost a hundred criminals—the worst of the worst—inside. *Would they wait for me and beat me up?* Or maybe their revenge would be sweet and silent. Seeing me rot behind bars would be enough, I imagine.

"The judge and the jury find Detective Winston innocent." She closed the letter and I could feel myself visibly relax. Maxine and the Kalman stood up and hugged, while Carrie silently nodded to me and slipped away. She was never an ally, anyway.

"Thank god," Ashbery breathed out and smiled at me. I shook Robert's hand, and suddenly I felt all three of them hugging me. I was still cuffed and wearing that atrocious orange colour, but I welcomed the hug. I honestly couldn't remember the last time I could feel a human's warmth so close to my own body. Maybe that time I was carrying Maxine upstairs when she was so drunk.

A couple of guards came closer to me, and while I thought they would take me back to the station, they just uncuffed me.

I looked at Maxine with a puzzled expression, wondering how many strings she pulled to get me out of there with such ease. I think she understood the awkwardness of my turning up at the station where people hated me.

"It wasn't me. I don't know why you look so surprised." She pointed a finger in the direction of the exit and I saw Bran standing there with a clear plastic bag of all possessions I had on me. I could see a pack of red Marlborough cigarettes and the small silver necklace I used to wear.

"You people are wonderful." I forced a smile on my face and went closer to Bran who was smiling back at me.

"I told him you were innocent. We all know you are," Maxine said, as I grabbed my possessions and whipped out my cigarettes.

I handed everyone one and looked in the pockets of my jeans, but there was no lighter. Someone must've taken it when I was getting processed and catalogued it as a dangerous weapon. Pigs.

"I'm afraid I don't have a light…" While I was talking, Maxine brought her silver lighter to my cigarette and I almost coughed from the surprise. She was grinning like a Cheshire cat.

"Your partner knows you better than anyone, right?" She smirked and I threw my head back, laughing. Only if she knew.

Later that evening, I invited everyone out for a celebratory beer. Ashbery came with his new girlfriend and we were introduced. I could see the spark in his eyes when he spoke to her, or when she spoke up. I was happy for them both.

Maxine grabbed my hand and led me to a dark corner of the bar.

"I need you to be cruelly honest with me, right now," she demanded and I nodded. I had a small plastic cup filled with beer, but I could see she wasn't drinking at all. I think she thought if I was drunk, I would pour my feelings out for her.

Wrong.

"Promise me you aren't hiding anything else. No more secrets."

"I promise." She held up her little finger and made me promise I wouldn't ever keep anything from her.

"God, what would I do without you?" She smiled as I grabbed her hand and led her back to the bar.

"One smart person once told me that change is inevitable. But I promise I won't lie to you again." I kissed her cheek and brought her and the new Mrs Ashbery to dance.

And what kind of a partner would I be if I *broke my promise*?

Chapter 17
Dear Maxine

Somewhere in Western Sahara

Dear Maxine,

It is day 42 of running. I hate to call this running though—it's the exact opposite. I'd tell you where I am, but what would be the fun of that?

The last time you saw me was at the celebration of my release.

That will also be the last time you ever see me.

No matter how deep you dig, no matter whom you question or track down, you won't be able to find me.

I am not Winston. I was truly never Winston.

Two months ago, during the flight home from Wyoming, Bran handed me my freedom card. Everything I've ever done wrong, all of my crimes, were there. And now they're gone.

You will never know what I did. I can tell you about all of my crimes—but I would lie. I'd lie and tell you they were buried in someone's backyard, but you aren't ready to hear what kind of animal I am.

Truthfully, this had been planned years in advance. There isn't a small detail I didn't plan. I know the answers to all the questions you have.

I got myself arrested; I organised this whole trial years before you even knew me.

Bran wasn't involved—he just followed the small crumbs I left for him. Smart boy, I must give that to him. I was so sure he would figure it out, being a genius, but he didn't. He even gave me the evidence of my presumed first crime. He was too naïve. Maybe this will finally bring you closer together.

I only have a few pages of paper, so I won't bore you with the details.

I left the party; I swore I was sick from all the stress and relief at the same time. You were so kind to offer help, but as always, I refused. I packed one bag. There is nothing else personal in that apartment, so don't waste your time going through my belongings. They don't mean anything. Each time you came inside and asked why I chose this certain carpet or pointed to all the pictures, just know it was all lies. But to be honest, *what isn't?*

My abuse story isn't—the scars I showed you were real. The story you heard in court was partially true. The dates and the people involved weren't true, but I tried to at least make my story close.

I killed more people than you think. Please find all the bodies before you try to find closure.

Hating me more will help.

I'd like to think of myself as a lesson for you. Don't ever trust someone—the only person you can trust is yourself. No matter who looks innocent, chances are they aren't. You are still young, so you'll learn it the easy way—you might cry and hate me, but after a couple of years or decades, you will see why I did what I did and how right I was for doing it.

That moment, when I slipped in court, was planned. For a second, you stilled and I swore you could see through me. It would've been more fun if you came after me. I love the chase after all, don't I?

Did I feel guilty? No.

See, when you live through as much as I did, the guilt vanishes after a while.

For lying to you, maybe a little.

You were so young when I first met you—remember standing there at the police station like a lost puppy? I was the one who got you that internship. You were the best in your class—hell, you were the best student in the whole police academy. When I saw you, with your thick glasses and that attitude, I knew you were the perfect victim for me.

Yes, I think you should also count as one of my victims—although I didn't kill you physically, I killed the idea of myself in your head, which might hurt even more than a bullet or a stab wound. You deserve a pat on the back for keeping up with me though. I gave you such a hard time and you never requested a break.

I hope you won't hate me too much to keep searching for my victims.

That's what's wrong with you.

No matter how cold you act, the death of your father impacted you well beyond how the average person can see. You carry the immense guilt for his death—you feel as if you could've done more.

I heard he was a good man.

Maybe I killed him too. *We'll never know.*

Your first question would probably be why. And to that, I have no answer. Maybe I do, but I prefer to keep you in the dark.

I'm not a sociopath—don't call me that. It's an insult.

I am just calculating. I can also guess you're biting your nails and your eyebrows are creased. Invest in a retinol cream for that.

Sometimes there is no why. For some people, it's just an urge. It's like an itch they cannot reach on their back. They wriggle and almost break their arms to scratch it, but they can't reach it. The next best thing would be to cut it.

I invaded your life like cancer. I grew slowly, so incredibly slow that you wouldn't be able to tell I'm even inside of your brain. I let you think you were special, I made you my partner. When I met you, you succumbed to the fantasy that I was the perfect role model.

You took so much liking to me, that at some point you will become me—it's inevitable.

You'll try not to be like me. Maybe you will finally go to therapy and talk all your issues out, but the truth is, nothing will save you. You were in too deep to climb out. I gave you an ultimatum, but you completely ignored it.

You won't ever fall in love. You won't ever find another family. You won't ever have kids. You won't have a nice life. You won't find someone who loves you like I do.

Each minute I spent with you, I felt like DaVinci when he created David.

You were so perfect.

You never questioned me and at first, you were afraid to come too close to me. I think all those years ago your intuition told you I'm dangerous. You should've listened.

But, unlike David, you weren't perfect. You were lazy.

You stopped asking the good questions. You just accepted me with open arms—no matter if I was a killer or not. You should've despised me.

You were average.

Nothing special.

Maybe you even liked me at the end.

So much *wasted* potential.

But life goes on.

Your second question will be how.

How did I manage to leave? How is it that no one stopped me? How did no one know?

It's simple, really. The tickets were booked a long time ago. I made sure it didn't look suspicious. I flew somewhere like Paris or Rome—a place where I would be unrecognisable. I made sure that I only investigated and therefore publicly existed in the United States. People in Europe had no idea who I was.

Isn't that funny? We as cops should make sure the perp doesn't get away.

I even found a guy who has this small plane that can take me anywhere in Europe. This sounds too easy, doesn't it? But it truly was; I assure you.

I kept taking out 100 dollars each month, blaming it on groceries and the water bill getting too high. I did it for more than a decade. Each time, no one noticed. I'm sure the guys at the precinct checked my accounts twice for any suspicious activity.

That's how you get away in a shell; you need to be as low-key as possible.

No crazy money transfers as they show you in movies, everything must be cash. You must be alone, with as little luggage as possible. Travel light, always. Don't bring a gun; you can easily acquire one in third-world countries.

Don't talk, don't stare, and don't buy anything out of the ordinary. Luxury logos draw attention. Get a fake passport and visa—teenagers these days make fakes quite cheap. Make sure you speak English and another language. Locals won't understand you.

Find a small place to live in, the cheaper the better. Switch countries every two months—make it two weeks after leaving from New York. Avoid gatherings and parties where people take pictures of you. No internet and no phones—no checking your emails or Instagram. Buy groceries locally, don't even think about going to a mall—there are too many cameras.

Don't make friends. Running away is a lonely journey, after all. No calling your mom or Bran. I'm sure Bran will put a small tracker in your phone after hearing the news about me.

He and I both know which path you will take.

Make sure you leave your apartment spotless. Drown the computer in acid and throw out the phone. Smash the place, if you have enough time, but mop all the hair and bleach the showers and sinks. Leave no food in the fridge. That will make people think you left a lot earlier. Delete everything off your phone before throwing it out. No pictures, no passwords, and no internet history. You'd be surprised how easy it is to hack your phone even when it lies at the bottom of a random trashcan in New York.

Don't buy a burner phone. Buy a book of maps, with cash. Make sure to pick a place where the population is low and not dense. Countries like Mongolia or Russia will be good for you. It's cold.

Make sure no one is following you. You'll be popular with the media for a while after I leave but at some point, the hype will die down and you will live normally.

Take out all your files at the doctor's office. Make sure there is absolutely nothing tying you to your old identity. Choose a random alias, nothing that connects your new name to your old name. Make up a new birthday and learn it. Make sure your brain understands you're not Maxine Johanssen anymore.

If you think you can stay living like Maxine Johanssen, you are wrong.

People like your mother or Kalman will try to find you. The easiest way for them to forgive you and forget you, is faking your death. Make sure it's not a coffin but a cremation instead. Buy the ash from the black market two years before you decide to die.

Never return to New York or the States.

Make sure to stay in Europe or Asia. After a while, move down to Africa, and then at last when you're older, move to a place like Denmark, where healthcare is good if you fall ill. If you're old enough, people won't recognise you. A smart choice would be to get plastic surgery, dye your hair, and get as many piercings as you can. Be unrecognisable.

If you start taking small amounts of cash out now, you could leave in five years. Maybe wait 10, so you can draw out as much as possible.

No matter what happens, never try to find me. If you do, I cannot assure you that you will be able to leave. I might even have to kill you and whoever you bring with you.

Never forget me, Maxine.

Never forget how good we were together and how special you felt and how I gave you enough of everything. I made you into the best version of yourself without you even knowing.

Take my cat, don't let her starve. Treat her kindly.

With love,

Winston.

Chapter 18
Mötet

He shouldn't be winning right now.

No matter how hard I try to find him, no matter how many clues he leaves me, I cannot find him. He jumps from continent to continent each week and never stays in a town for more than 24 hours. He's tactical—playing the game. He loved the game.

Cat and Mouse. *Him and Me.*

What would I even tell him if I saw him? Would I run to him and embrace him? Would I hate him more than I do now?

"You have to be careful, Maxine. You never know who can be hiding in the shadows." Winston murmured close to my ear as I held the gun and pointed it at the target.

"You should be careful. If I whip around, I could shoot you," I whispered the last part. Me and Winston met only a few weeks ago but he was growing fast on me. We found that we complemented each other well.

He was Yin, I was Yang.

"You would never."

"If you ever went rogue..." I fired the first shot into the dark alley.

"You have to. It's your job," Winston said with such ease, that it made me think this wasn't the first time he said this.

"You're never going rogue. You're a good person," I said as I fired the second shot.

And then the third.

And then came the fourth. Winston stayed silent, and I stopped asking questions. We just stared at the piece of paper which had three holes in its heart, and one in the head.

I was lying in bed. He haunted my dreams. I had realistic dreams where he would visit my apartment. I could no longer sleep for more than four hours, consecutively.

He's gone. It's impossible. My brain reminded me.

I can't lie. I was having a hard time. I started missing therapy and started packing 'emergency' bags in case a hint would drop.

I stopped answering calls—Ashbery almost broke down my door last Monday to see if I was still alive.

I was preparing for something I hoped would never come. I wished he would disappear. I wish I could live my life normally, without commission hearings and bullshit talks with Barnes.

I wish I never met him. My heart was frozen in my chest. I couldn't feel anymore. I was shallow and empty.

I was currently in the heart of France—Paris. I landed a couple of hours ago. I couldn't give a shit about the jet lag or the time difference; I needed to get to the Eiffel Tower as fast as I could.

Eighteen hours ago, I received a letter from Winston with a small Polaroid of the Eiffel Tower, presumably taken right in front of it.

Carrie and Ash had been calling non-stop. They found out I hadn't been in New York for almost a month, and they wanted to come along with me to find Winston. I declined, blocked their contacts, crushed my SIM card under the heel of my boot and kicked it from my balcony.

I took out the small Polaroid I received. I compared it to the Eiffel to see exactly where he stood. After a while of shuffling around, I was there.

It felt nostalgic to play this game.

I wondered if he was watching me right now—taking the smallest steps to see exactly where he stood like he was some artist.

He was.

The Eiffel Tower was truly beautiful. For a split second, the scene felt like a vacation—and then it stopped. I took a deep breath in, and out. From the corner of my eye, I saw a scrawny figure exit a black cab. He had brown sunglasses on and a long coat that masked what he was wearing underneath. I wouldn't be monitoring any stranger like this, but he was different.

He looked straight at me when I stood in a big crowd in front of the Eiffel.

Impossible. My breathing stopped for almost a minute—I was choking. I couldn't take a deep breath to save my life—that's how much he controlled me.

One look from him and I was dying.

We stood there, looking at each other. I was almost sure he was coming closer until I finally managed to take a deep breath and cough. Closing my eyes for only a split second, he slipped from my view. I looked around myself, turning in a full circle, but I couldn't see him anymore.

He's gone.

No.
No. No. Fuck.

I fucked up. Grabbing my bag from the floor, I threw it over my shoulder and charged full speed in the direction where he stood. I could feel people staring at me, but I couldn't give one fuck.

I ran. I went into random crowded streets that I didn't recognise.

I must look and sound crazy, but *I swear he was just there—right in front of me.*

I hit a small street car. I didn't stop. The man shouted some curses at me in French but I had my target in mind. Running and running, I finally thought I had him. Grabbing the man by the shoulder, I kicked his legs and he collapsed to the pavement.

Turning him over, I saw an unfamiliar face.

No.

I'm not crazy. I never was. I could swear Winston was just there. His cologne was still in the air, luring me like a prey to the predator. I stared at the man who screamed in pain but I couldn't bring myself to help him. I ran away from the scene as fast as I could before he could call the cops and have me sent back to New York.

"Life is never good, Maxine—We always have a new body in the morgue. We work so that criminals can't get away, but we will never be able to catch them all. Doesn't matter how much someone slips up, one day, there will be a criminal you will never be able to catch. No matter how long you will be looking for him, he will simply disappear. You won't be able to sleep. You won't have any appetite to eat. You won't love life the way you do now, because one day, this life will leave you empty and shallow and you will slowly die inside."

"Are you dying?" I asked.

"Every single day." He dragged the words out and looked outside of the window, ignoring my gaze.

I was not in New York, although I promised Ashbery I would go back; after dodging his numerous calls, I sent him a voicemail saying I was okay, and just needed some time. I was truthfully never going to return. New York sparked too many memories back to life—the precinct, our chess spot, where I was shot for the first time, the library where we met…

There were too many places that screamed Winston.

Instead, I landed at Gatwick and took the night train to Brighton.

I hated England—I hated the English people.

Their accent and that fake niceness were enough to make me gag sometimes, but it was the place that lured me in. I was carrying one suitcase, filled with my clothes and Winston's diaries. I hadn't opened them. I hadn't read one sentence. In fact, I was scared of what would be inside of them.

Would it be just case notes? Would there be small scribbles and drawings? Maybe even a card or a stain from his coffee.

Looking out of the window, I could feel my phone vibrate with a message tone.

"Page 88. Diary labelled 2009"—Unknown number

Shit.

I looked around myself—an older lady knitting, a short teenager, and a woman with the highest pair of heels I'd ever seen.

I placed the phone back on the table, thinking about my options.

I tried to call the number. After two rings, I was alerted by the monotonous voice of the call lady, saying that this number wasn't in service anymore.

So, he was alive. And had some sort of a phone. Great. Now he was just laughing at me.

I opened the diary labelled 2009 and counted the pages.

9
20
64
75
85
87
88
Here.

My mind wanted to see what was there—I was truly curious. But my hands shook, and I dropped the diary on the floor, and it closed.

I took that as a sign from the universe—*not yet.*

Chapter 19
Page 88

We Began Our Story in 2003

I was young and naive; he was ready to take complete advantage of me. 20 years later, the story changes.

I spent the last two years in hiding. I ensured everyone thought I was travelling through Europe but was still in New York. I never moved an inch. I was waiting for Winston to slip up; everyone makes mistakes, even him.

I monitored every single country. Every camera there was at the border was running face-matching software. Bran sat with me in my living room every day—if I can still call it my living room. I wasn't living in that room anymore. I was just watching people pass borders every day. I hardly slept—my dreams became nightmares very quickly. I didn't need to rest. I rested enough.

For months, not one face matched. I started losing hope, thinking he was smart enough to stay wherever he was. But I remembered I knew him. I knew how he thought and what he thought, I just didn't know where.

"You should take a shower." Bran pointed out the fact I'd been wearing the same shirt for almost a week. The material started smelling a long time ago, but I refused to stop looking at the screens. I was too afraid I might miss him.

Without looking up, I showed Bran my middle finger. I hardly cared about our friendship anymore. We weren't really friends—we were only looking forward to the same goal.

Catch Winston.

What happens after you catch him? My subconscious reminded me.

I had no idea.

After Paris, I was sure we were better off without him. I stopped looking for a couple of months, until Bran showed up and insisted we find him.

"So what, after months of searching you just gave up?" He laughed, demanding an answer.

"Yes, B. That's what happens after you lose your lead." I was tired of all the questions.

"That's not the Maxine I knew." He scoffed and looked away. I guess he despised me so much that he couldn't even look at me anymore.

"Fuck you," I snarled. "Do you know how it feels to be so close to catching him, and then he just magically disappears? I was this close." I pinched my fingers together.

"I was this close to touching him, Bran. I hate him. I really do, but I cannot drop everything and run after him forever."

"Not forever, just for a few more months. He will slip one day."

"I don't want to dedicate the rest of my life to him. You should understand me." My hands trembled when I reached to take a cigarette from my pocket.

"If we stop, he will roam free until he dies. That could be years. He could do so much more damage to the world." Bran ran a hand through his short hair.

"Can he?" I laughed hopelessly. He ruined so many lives—mine, his, Kalman's, and Carrie's.

After a beat of silence, I spoke again.

"He ruined us all, didn't he?"

Bran nodded slowly. I could see he wanted to say something, but he stayed silent.

The silence will drive us mad one day.

<u>*Two years later.*</u>

I will remember third of August forever. One second, I was opening the blinds to my living room—I got rid of all the screens and I was left with my computer, and I was smiling at the people passing in the streets of New York. I was still unemployed and my mother was still worried about me, but I was healing slowly. I only checked my computer once a day and I even started to write again. Life was suddenly feeling like spring again.

I kept messaging Bran and he kept updating me about the case, but I was happy Winston didn't make an appearance in the last two years. I wasn't angry anymore—I accepted this is what life would be like.

I made my way to the New York library. I kept looking over the shelves, noticing which ones had the most dust on them and I decked my books on the small trolly. Life was good. I picked up an old copy of Plath's poems but refrained from picking up Hughes, who was Winston's favourite. He kept saying nature was better than confessions. I guess we were really *that* different.

I sat down in one of the creaking chairs. I adopted my seat and sat in it every Monday. I kept my schedule busy, so I wouldn't fall into checking the cameras four times per day again. I stopped smoking cigarettes and started to travel again without worrying I might run into Winston again.

Opening the book, I randomly chose a poem and started reading.

Peel off the napkin O my enemy.
Do I terrify? ——
The nose, the eye pits, the full set of teeth? The sour breath will vanish in a day.
Soon, soon the flesh
The grave cave ate will be At home on me
And I a smiling woman.
I am only thirty.
And like the cat, I have nine times to die.

"You know I hate Plath," a voice behind me startled me. It was old and croaky, almost like the man had been smoking for more than 30 years.

I whipped around, but the sun was shining in my face and I couldn't see anything. I squinted my eyes—a taller man, older, perhaps in his 60s with a dark blue coat.

"You look good," he spoke again, and I finally connected the voice to who this was.

"Winston." With shaky breaths, I jumped up from the chair and grabbed my gun from my belt hoist.

"Now, let's not jump to conclusions. We should talk. It's been a long time."

He was clever. There were no cameras in the library. There were hardly any people at this time in the morning.

"How did you get to America?" I tried to remain calm and collected.

"I never really left, did I?" He smirked.

"No. You sent me letters from Europe and I saw you in Paris."

"Paris? Oh god, no. You know how much I hate the French." He laughed. I stayed calm, with my gun trained on him.

He looked bad. He was skinnier than the last time I saw him, and his hair was almost all grey. I couldn't believe my sight. Was he here?

"So who was it in Paris?" I mumbled. My mind was running 10,000 kilometres of data and information, trying to understand him.

"Were you really in Paris?" His face changed suddenly. His skin was soggier and more mature. He aged ten years within seconds.

"Yes, I went to Paris. Three years ago." He took a step forward, and another one until the barrel of my gun was touching his chest.

"Are you sure?" His face aged faster. He looked 100 years old, ready to die.

"Yes!" I screamed at him. As soon as I screamed, he dropped to the floor and lay there motionless.

I shot up from my bed. I could feel small beads of sweat running down my back and soaking up into my pyjama bottoms. Looking around me, I made sure no one was in my room. I fell back down into my pillow and tried to catch my breath. The night terrors were getting more realistic each night. I looked at my nightstand and grabbed my phone.

3:48—Might as well get up.

I gathered my two most important belongings—my gun and my phone. I rented a small cottage close to the Seven Sisters cliffs. They were truly beautiful, and even more calming than my balcony overlooking the busy streets of New York.

No one knew me here. No reporters, no police staff who looked at me and whispered under their breaths. There was no one I knew. I was completely alone.

I ran outside, breathed in fresh air, and didn't bother locking my doors. I lived completely remote. The nearest person to me was an older woman with her big white dog.

I ran as fast as I could, almost as if someone was chasing me. Closing my eyes, I trusted my feet to take me where I wanted to be. I could hear the grasshoppers twinkle, but I was in complete darkness. If someone was watching over me I wouldn't know.

What would happen if I didn't stop and ran out of ground? How long would I fall for? Would it hurt? I was debating ending my life while running as fast as I could.

Would I feel free?

No. I stopped suddenly as my eyes snapped open, a couple of metres away from the end of the cliff. I was breathing hard, but for a couple of minutes, I felt free.

From a distance, my eyes caught a small twinkle in the moonlight. I came closer, using my phone to locate this small object. A small silver coin shined light in the middle of the grass. I grabbed the coin and inspected it. It had Roman numerals and was crooked around the edges. It must've been old. *Lucky.*

"Lucky," I said to myself quietly, the corners of my mouth turning up slowly.

"You are, aren't you?" A voice startled me—and I turned around as fast as I could.

"No, no not again." I closed my eyes and rubbed them as hard as I could. Opening my eyes again, I saw him still, looking like himself. He wasn't aging. He didn't look like a corpse. He was looking...*real.*

"Pinch yourself," he commanded with a stern voice and I obliged.

I pinched the skin on my hand between my fingers as hard as I could. Closing my eyes, I breathed out and opened my eyes again.

He was still there.

"No. You're not real," I chanted like a prayer.

Winston came closer to me, touched my hand, and held it. The rough skin on his hands, the way he held my hand—It was him.

"No." I had tears in the corners of my eyes.

"Yes. I'm here and I'm real." He wanted to embrace me, but I ripped my hand from his grasp.

"Get the fuck away from me. Don't you dare?"

"I came back for you."

"For me?" I let out a hopeless laugh, looking at the sky above me. "Are you sick? It's been years, Winston. Years of me trying to find you and kill you. Bastard." I gritted my teeth.

"We have to leave, Maxine."

"No. You have to leave." I looked at him—all I could see was his silhouette.

"Don't make me shout. Let's go."

"Do I look like I'm going to go with you? I hate you." He shook his head.

"Maxine, don't you see? We *are* the same. I ran away, and you did too." He pointed to me. "We are the same," he said it like he believed it.

"No." I tried to grab the gun in my waistband, but couldn't find it. Looking around myself, I didn't see it. It must've fallen out.

"Look at yourself. Look at you. You were fired; you were kicked out like an orphan. And you ended up here, in the middle of nowhere in England. I'm offering you the last chance."

"Join the cold-blooded killers club?" I spat out.

"Join the winners," he boasted as if he was going to change my opinion.

"You're stupid if you think I will let you leave. You're going behind bars for the rest of your life. The only winner you will be will be in brawls with other idiots. I will get you." I swung my hands and hit him square in the jaw. He recoiled, spat out some blood, and rolled his shoulders back, ready to hit me back.

"Fuck. You still have a good right hook. I guess things didn't change much." He charged for my head but I was quick. Kicking his stomach, he dropped to his knees.

"You should be begging for my forgiveness," I grit out.

"You failed at trying to find me." Punch. Missed. "You failed at your job." Another missed attempt at hitting me.

"You failed me." To this, I froze and got hit in my jaw. "You are a failure," he screamed.

I didn't hesitate in the next second. I stood up on my shaky legs and ran as fast as I could in his direction. I rammed into his body and shoved him as far and as hard as I could.

He stumbled back and disappeared over the horizon of the rising sun.

The last thing I heard was his pathetic attempt at calling out my name.

He was gone. *Forever*.

I fell to my knees and looked at the orange sun illuminating the sky.

"So, this is what freedom tastes like." I told myself, wiping the sweat from my forehead. I could feel my heart beat again, I could feel my body filling up with blood, I could feel the taste of my tongue in my mouth.

I was finally free.

Chapter 20
The End

"Your first kill will be the hardest." Winston drank a shot of vodka and shivered. We were sitting in a run-down bar, somewhere in Siberia. Our planes were leaving in 19 hours.

We had 19 hours to come up with a plan on how to kill me.

Figuratively, of course.

I was going into hiding. My life wasn't mine anymore. The media was monitoring my every move. I still hated Winston, I still despised him, but I couldn't live like this anymore.

I would never be a criminal like him. I had no idea how someone could become one. But the truth is I would rather be dead than alive. I needed a fresh start.

"So, I do all the things you told me in the letter, right? What's next?" I signalled for the bartender to pour us another shot. I was in desperate need of alcohol to get through this conversation.

"You have to disappear. Completely. Call no one. Make sure Bran cannot find you. If he can, and you find me, I will have to kill both of you."

"I understand."

"Do you? Because this means that Maxine Johannes will no longer exist. There is no way you can abandon your life and come back to it. Absolutely no way. This is your choice—

I'm not pressuring you, but know this; you will never be the same after this. You will be lonely and desperate to go back, but you cannot. You will be dead. Buried or burned, and gone."

"When do I die?"

I died in August 2025. One day after I 'killed' Winston, I wrote a suicide letter and Winston brought a dead rotting body into my small cottage.

"Fuck, this smells."

"She, she smells."

"Where do you even get a dead body?" I coughed and held my fist to my mouth.

"Don't ask." Winston dragged her close to the bathtub and I could hear her organs mushing inside of her bloated body.

"How did you even think of this?" I left the bathroom and gagged.

"Maxine. I told you this was all planned before we even knew each other."

"You know you would find me?"

"I had an idea I would meet someone who I won't be able to get rid of." He smiled at me, but I was still reluctant.

He was still a killer, my brain reminded me.

But he loved me. He loved me more than anyone else in the world.

"Should I pack my stuff?" I asked.

"No. We're burning it." *Oh.* "And get undressed. We're burning your clothes too." *Fucking hell.*

Sitting in Winston's old plane, I couldn't stop thinking about why he would help me. I knew he killed all those people, I knew which body hid where, yet I was still alive.

"Stop thinking so hard." Winston laid down his newspaper, neatly folded.

"I'm not," I lied. He knew. I knew he knew.

"Are you happy now?"

"No."

"Why?" He lit a cigarette with a Russian logo on the packet.

"'You will never know true happiness'—don't you remember?" I rolled my eyes and kept looking out of the window.

"I know you. You will be happy when we start to live again. You've been existing for so many years; it's time to live—to enjoy life lavishly and loudly. To explore the world. No more jobs or killers. We put so many of them behind bars; it's time for that vacation." He chuckled and handed me his cigarette.

"Not nearly enough," I whispered—he knew what I meant. I meant that he was still free. "How come you don't get to rot behind bars for all the hellish things you did? How come you get to swim, while others drown?" I exhaled the smoke into the cabin.

"I deserve it. I have been through so many bad things in life that I cannot just survive anymore. You shouldn't judge me. You did your share of bad things." He scoffed at my attempt to insult him.

"I had done nothing wrong." I shook my head and Winston laughed.

"Yes. You knew what I was all these years. Even when we met, you turned a blind eye to me. I gave you so many hints—I wanted to corrupt you into a better version of yourself. I left signs, and I left you with questions yet you never asked. Why? Are you so dumb that you couldn't see?" He grabbed the cigarette from my fingers and put it out.

"I had no idea. You were mysterious, yes, but never have I even thought that you could be a cold-blooded murderer. You fucking go around and pretend you're the smartest person but you don't know me."

"I know you better than you know yourself."

"Stop lying! You never knew, you never cared. God, you are insufferable." I gritted out.

"Am I insufferable because you despise me? Or am I insufferable because you see yourself in me? I know you'd do the same thing I did. I know you hate me, but you also hate yourself. You always did. That's why you succumbed to me so easily."

"I never succumbed. I am my own self." I tried to hit him, but he grabbed my hand.

"You hit me, but you also hit yourself. We are one, Maxine. We think the same thoughts; we know the same things…"

"Where are the bodies? Tell me."

"Oh." He laughed. "This again. Is this why you came on this plane? You gave up your life to know my secret?"

"No." I shook my head.

"Then who are you now? Where is Maxine?"

"Sitting right fucking in front of you."

"Really? Are you sure?" He smirked.

No. Yes. Maybe.

"Yes. I am still myself."

"Maxine doesn't exist anymore. She's dead. You are nameless. You have no family, no friends, and no home. We are the same now Max. Or should I call you by another name?" He raised his eyebrows.

"You think you won?" I asked him. "You think you are a God? You are mortal. One shot from my gun and you are dead. No one will ever find you. We're on top of a frozen forest. There's no chance." I leaned closer to him. "We are dead now. Whatever I do to you, will never be found."

"You want to kill me?" He grabbed his duffle bag and opened it. Inside, a piece of shiny metal caught my attention.

He placed a *gun* between us.

He placed a *loaded* gun between us.

"Kill me. Go ahead. I won't blame you. I ruined your life, didn't I?" He cocked his head. "But remember. You won't make it in this storm without me."

I wasted no time, no breath, and no thoughts and reached for the gun. Winston didn't grab my hand now—he didn't stop me.

"Why do you want to die so much?"

"Kill me or don't, no questions asked." He folded his hands into his lap and sat quietly.

"I want answers."

"You won't ever get them."

I fired a shot into the seat next to him.

"Remember, I don't have to kill you with *one* shot."

"Go on, torture me. I won't say one word. You're not good enough to be trusted with my secret."

"And she was?"

"Who?"

"Carrie Heller Jones. Your ex-wife. She told me what you told her two minutes after she got her letter. You should've been a poet, you know? Could've gotten money for that talent to lie straight to her face."

"I never told her anything."

"27 February 1999. You told her about body number seven. It took her twenty years to figure it out, but there's a body in Ashbery's morgue and he's cutting its skin open to find out what's hiding beneath." I nodded, keeping my gun trained on him.

"I will give you two choices. Either you tell me the truth and I will bury that body with your DNA, or you will tell me the truth and I will kill you."

"I want a deal. With you."

"Fuck you."

"Kill me then," He threw his hands up. "I have nothing to hide. How come you think she didn't lie? You trust her more than me?"

"You have two minutes to tell me what happened. I want the truth."

"Okay."

For the next minute, he stayed quiet. All I could hear was the whirring of the plane.

"One minute left."

"You're impatient." Winston chuckled.

"You're dead in 50 seconds."

"Thank god, it was about time." He stuck a hand into his duffle bag and pulled out a paper, which looked 40 years old.

"This is why I did it." He pointed to a small picture in the right corner of the newspaper. A small picture of a boy from the 70s was plastered with a bulk of text.

"This isn't you."

"No. It's my brother. He was killed by his foster parents in an 'accident'. They never served one day in jail in their life for it. They killed him. He was six years old when he died."

"Why should I believe you and this sob story?"

"Your father killed him. He was the foster parent, along with his wife."

"Bullshit. My father died years ago." I was close to pulling the trigger.

"Did he? Or did your mother tell you that? I'm sure there must've been a funeral then?"

He was playing with me, but I couldn't help to wonder if what he was saying was true. My mother always said my father was a bad man, but never to this extent.

"So your brother died, now you have the right to kill people?"

"So your father died, and now you have the right to kill people? Yes, I do, and yes you do. This world is filled with people who don't deserve to be here. We do. We're in charge of making sure everyone who isn't supposed to be here isn't here." He shrugged his shoulders in a calm manner—I had a gun trained on him and he was *calm*.

"Maybe we don't deserve to be here. Maybe we should die. Maybe the world would be a better place."

"Too many maybes. Focus on facts," he reminded me. I chuckled.

Taking a deep breath, I said my last words to Winston.

"You don't deserve to be here. You should die. The world will be a better place," I chanted.

"Exactly. Smart girl." He straightened up, thinking I would lower my gun, but I didn't move.

"Goodbye, Winston." His eyes widened.
And one shot from the gun rang in the cabin.

Goodbye.

Chapter 21
Epilogue

30 May 2009

Dear Maxine,

I have sinned.

I hope you can forgive me.

I hope one day, I will grow old next to you—but now, I guess you found out about who I am. I am truly sorry it had to go this way, but I can't say I found another way. I was desperate to find a way to leave my past and focus on my present. If we had met sooner, you'd understand.

I am a liar. Please blame me for everything.

One last thing.

There is a dead body, somewhere, with your set of DNA and fingerprints that I have collected of you when you were sleeping on my couch.

It's a woman, looking just like you, and I have killed her for you. You were meant to be the only woman in my life.

I hope you can forgive me for this, but it had to be done. With love, Winston.

THE END

Chapter 22
Final Article

Shocking Twist: NYPD Discovers Detective Johannes' Fingerprints on Deceased Body.
By: Charlotte Masar

In a stunning turn of events, the New York City Police Department has found itself amid a gripping mystery as one of its ex-detectives, Maxine Johannes, has been implicated in a homicide case. The discovery of Detective Johannes' fingerprints on a deceased body has sent shock waves through the law enforcement community and left the public clamouring for answers.

The unsettling revelation came to light during a routine investigation into a recent homicide in an undisclosed location in New York City. The victim, identified as a 35-year-old female, was found in a deserted alleyway, prompting the NYPD to launch a thorough examination of the crime scene.

During the meticulous collection of evidence, forensic experts uncovered a shocking detail—the fingerprints of ex-Detective Johannes, a seasoned and respected member of the force, were present on the deceased body. This unexpected twist has thrown the investigation into disarray, leaving both law enforcement officials and the public in a state of disbelief.